The Enchanted Books

AND THE LAND OF PHANTOMS

A.AVYUKT, RITVIK KRISHNA.R

Books in the series

The Enchanted Books and The Villain's Escape,

The Enchanted Books and The Wrath Of The Master

The Enchanted Books and The Land of Phantoms

(In reading order)

The winter winds had already started as there was mist blocking the roads. The family knew that a haughty winter was on its way. They had no worries except to sip their hot coffees and rest on their couch. The last few months were quite relaxed and smooth after the quest in Olympia, but they did expect something peculiar from their Olympia, considering the mind set of Thunder. School, spending the weekend with their family, everything a normal family could have. All these events were sailing smooth until there was a knock at the door. A knock which was another call. Now they were invited back to Olympia, but the other hemisphere of it, also the dark side, was wickedly known as *The Land Of Phantoms.*

TABLE OF CONTENTS

~CHAPTER ONE~

A Bad Day

This wasn't the best morning for the family. It all started when Jay spilled a whole cup of tea on his shirt, Gita let her toast burn and Bingo forgot to throw the clothes into the washing machine. It was a classic Ramsay morning. However, the situation got back to normal pretty quickly and everyone just began to carry on with their regular routines.

Bingo had just cooked breakfast, which was toast and jam with a glass of orange juice for each person. He wasn't always a great cook, but he had developed the skill gradually after the incident at Mount St. Helena two and a half years ago. Gita arranged the plates neatly in order, as Bingo collected the day's newspaper. Bingo used to be an avid newspaper reader, but had stopped because he developed an opinion that "The Media is nothing but lies" and that "It spreads all fake news to lure the readers into believing its lies". Even though he hated it, he always gave a read through the headlines, just to keep up with the news around the world. He was about to close the newspaper, when an article caught his eye.

"STOMING RETURNS"

"A.B.A Stoming, the murderer has been sighted once more after a few months. A few rumors say that the murder of the family at Chicago was planned and

executed by none other than him. The president urged the citizens to not go into mindless panic, and leave it to the government to handle. A few other nations have also claimed sightings of the criminal. However, it is important to remember, that when Stoming was sighted four months ago, nothing bad had happened. Has Stoming gone silent? Or is he planning something big?

-Anna Parker."

Bingo folded the newspaper and kept it on the coffee table. 'The media just wants stories,' he commented. 'He is on another planet, for god's sake.'

Jay came in after changing his shirt. He looked at the article as he sipped his orange juice. 'Well, why did you read it?'

'If you knew it was all fake news?'

Polskite the griffin, well, an owl now, screeched and hooted as if he was angry too. The family, especially Bingo, had developed a strong bond with the griffin the year before. Polskite had saved their lives numerous times, the thought of what would have happened without the creature still haunted them. They had been thinking of a shorter nickname, and decided to name him 'Poly'. Even though it sounded like a parrot's name, the family got used to it.

Bingo petted Poly gently.

They knew the news was fake. After all, these were dark times. The people they trusted, could turn against them any time. To the U.S Government, Stoming was just a cold-blooded criminal who went on killing people, and they were once true. That was what the family thought about the man. Stoming was a puppet in the hands of Thunder, until he was betrayed by his own "Master". They never knew when he could become loyal again to the King of Olympia.

Poly scooted back to his cage, tucking his beak straight into his bowl of assorted nuts, his own nutritious feast which was kept ready for him, every morning. The original diet of griffins in Olympia normally was of *Rabkeys,* and some giant caterpillars. Obviously they couldn't feed the owl Rabbits and caterpillars, but they were fortunate that the creature had developed an interest in nuts.

Just then, Gita entered the room, taking a big bite off her peanut butter toast. She stood rigid, as she caught sight of the newspaper which Bingo had placed open on the table.

Jay was quietly getting ready by dumping the supplies in his bag and slinging it over his shoulder. He was really not cheerful.

Gita was finished packing and was ready to go.

'Jay you sure you're okay?' asked Bingo, looking at his long face.

Jay nodded. 'I'm okay, dad. Don't worry.'

The house was filled with conjecture, with everyone packing their bags for work. The only one who was calm and asleep was Cookie, their Golden Retriever whom they had rescued last year. They were pretty sure that Cookie was the perfect dog. However, Cookie and Poly were not what you call "Best Buddies", but they certainly made things work out between them.

Meanwhile, Bingo had recently interviewed and got a job at a famous science lab, which offered a better position and a good pay. However, he deserved it for his hard work and perseverance.

Gita and Jay walked out of the house with their backpacks as Bingo checked on Cookie and Poly once again. After a quick minute, Bingo came out, his car keys in one hand and a black backpack on his shoulder. The three looked at the house opposite to theirs and heard a bit of noise coming from the interior of the house. Ramesh had come out of the house and was shouting at his children to hurry up. Gita chuckled at the sight. 'Looks like they're late again!'

Jay grinned. 'Yep. It happens almost every day.'

Bingo got into the car. 'You better start if *you* don't want to be late.' He started the Honda Civic with a soft purr. Cookie barked and Poly hooted from the window as the car started moving. They reached the school and Jay and Gita got down, and slowly walked towards the gate. The cousins attended Oak Hill Elementary and Jay and Gita attended Oak Hills Junior High. The cousins thought that it was awesome that their schools were right next to each other, and that they could visit Jay and Gita anytime, but that wasn't the case. However Jay felt it was his luck that they didn't let the kids out, or it would have been a zoo there. He walked past the Notice Board, and got to know that it was "Open Day". Anyway, who cares? It was going to be Bingo again. It was indeed quite odd with kids bringing both their parents, while Jay went along with Bingo. Most kids didn't want their parents to come along, but Jay was different. To be frank, it was quite embarrassing for Bingo the last time.

Jay walked into his class with his school bag hanging on his shoulder, he was welcomed with none other than a bunch of young bullies of his age who teased him for almost every little thing.

'OH NO!' a voice spoke. It reeked of sarcasm. It was Oliver. Just as all schools had its own collection of stupid, proud bullies, Oliver was an asset for the "BULLY ASSOCIATION."

One day, Jay had blurted out the Olympia incident. It slipped out of Jay's mouth when the bullies were gloating about their recent "acts of bravery", which most of the time, were actually going past the Principal Office without getting caught, and bullying the fifth grade students. He sat down near his friend, Zen as he mostly ignored what the bullies were saying.

The class was still noisy, and Jay still hadn't figured out what was so important. He heard the same voice again, but this time, it was directed at him.

'Oh! Has Jay remembered the maths test, or was he staying up late, doing nothing?' mocked Oliver.

'Maths test?' Jay still had no clue. Suddenly, it struck him. *Oh no. It was Mrs. Tam's Math Quiz!* The thought of the Math quiz was not so frightening. But it was *Mrs. Tam's Quiz.* Just as Jay tried to take in the shock, Oliver pitched in *again.*

'Shocked, eh?' Whenever he talked, his nostrils grew larger, which was just a plain disgusting sight.

'Uh…' stuttered Jay. He had no time to worry about the creature that was standing in front of him, he had to think of what he was going to do to survive the test.

'I know the reason why he didn't study! He must've been trying to build the story of….what is it?'

'Olympia!' Another boy finished the sentence.

Oliver chuckled and agreed. 'How do his parents manage this load of rubbish?' he added. 'Oh, right, even his mother is dead. I feel bad for his dad.'

'Like father, like son, right?' another boy added.

The two boys chuckled.

Now, Jay can take any insult about him, but he couldn't bear it if someone insults his family. He really wanted to punch Oliver in the face, but he had no time.

'Shut up, will you?' said Zen, his one and only friend.

Zen was not the type you'd generally find. He was weird in his own way but was a good guy who stood for his friends. He was also a similar boy like Jay, who had lost his father when he was little. When Zen was a mere toddler, his father had disappeared and he had been living with his mother since in his simple wooden cottage. Whenever he asked his mother about this, she was too emotional to talk about it.

The incident didn't have an impact on Zen at all, he was not at an age to accept it. But he still had a ray of hope, if his father would be alive and safe, even though not with them, but somewhere. On the other hand he knew it was too good to be true. His father was gone. He was never coming back.

'Don't you have any other work to do Oliver?' retorted Jay, shoving the stuff back into his backpack. He was quite used to these snarky comments.

Suddenly, the class grew silent, the second when a stern face entered the room. Students scurried off to their desks, the class filled with the sounds of hushed whispers. Finally, an old woman, in her early sixties, walked in. Her eyes looked as sharp as a hawk, as if she could spot a student cheating miles away. Her dark, brown hair was tied in a bun, the wrinkles on her face made her look more experienced and *scary*. Mrs. Tam was a wonderful teacher, but she was extremely strict and vigilant. She was supposed to retire years ago, but the school had retained her on the basis of her performance. Jay reckoned that she would be a permanent asset of the school. Mrs. Tam slowly strided into the room, holding a thick bundle of question papers in her hand and went to the teacher's desk. Taking off the rubber band of the papers, she started distributing them to every student. She was at the other end of the classroom as Jay tried his best to remember all the formulas.

Mrs. Tam arrived at Jay's desk. 'You better attend all the questions.' She handed over a sheet to Jay. All students started answering the questions once the teacher gave them the instruction. Jay started answering as well. He was extremely confident for the first few questions because he did practise a little. Even if he didn't want to, Bingo made him do so. He couldn't deny the fact it was cool having a parent who was an expert at science, as his homework was sorted every day. It was also quite fun doing his homework with his dad, as Bingo would criticise the syllabus and the "way of teaching" nowadays, and would keep going about how the teachers have to be more strict. Jay totally didn't agree to that, he says Bingo would know his pain only if he attended his math class. But as the test went on, Jay's pace decreased as he struggled to remember how to show his working. This was exactly how every test he took shaped out. The clock was ticking as fast as ever, and the teacher had been frantically checking her watch every ten seconds. One hour had passed. Mrs. Tam stood up from her seat, took one last glance at her watch, as she proceeded to the first bench. Of course, the brainy first benchers were done almost half-an-hour ago, and proudly turned their papers over. Jay, who was racing to finish all the questions, was comparatively lucky, as he was sitting in the last bench. Mrs. Tam was almost into the last row, keeping a close watch on Jay who had two more questions left.

'Paper?'

'Just a minute Ma'am,' he replied, his hand throbbing.

'I asked for your paper,' repeated Mrs. Tam.

This time, her voice was sterner. Jay was trying to finish his paper but at the same time, he knew that he couldn't get Mrs. Tam too angry. It didn't need a genius to know what would happen if he did. But Mrs. Tam didn't give him more time. She pulled the paper from his hands and added it to the bundle. Finally, the exam was over. People sighed and boasted around the class. You see, Jay's class was a unique assortment. There were the bullies, Oliver and his allies, the nerds, as they call them, the kids who would sacrifice their vacations to study, the rich kids, who went on gloating about their belongings, and finally, the innocent, which only consisted of Jay and his best friend, Zen. He slowly exited the classroom, careful not to get into any more trouble. He got out and saw his timetable. Yes! Finally! A class he loved. Art. He loved Art, not just for the subject, but also because the new teacher was so kind and helpful, unlike the others who look like they descended from the fates. To top it all, he could do anything he wanted. Usually, he would doodle the whole time, which he knew was not wrong, as it was "ART" too.

The day passed by slowly. Finally, it was time for the last class. The most nervous and awaited one. The class when all the students were supposed to receive their answer papers for the test which they wrote in the morning. The entire classroom was filled with nervous-talks and murmurs which all died as Mrs. Tam entered the room, with a bundle of papers in her right hand. Resting on the teachers' chair with a short, evil-like grin, she kept the papers down. Give her a scepter and a few powers, she could be the next Thunder.

Mrs Tam opened her assessment sheet to check the average scores. She gave a faint smile which was quite rare. 'This exam was extremely easy, which made me guess that it was the reason the majority had scored well.'

Easy? Lady, you must be kidding.

She started reading from the assessment sheets before she gave out the papers. The people who got high marks were called out using the sheet, followed by some silent cheering.

'Aiden,' she called. 'Ninety nine. An A+. Good job, young man.'

Aiden punched the air in joy as Mrs. Tam started handing the papers as well to the people she announced. The papers were given. Mixed reactions were seen in the class, both by the students and the teacher. A few more papers were distributed, and the next was Jay. He slowly stood up from his seat, and tried his best to remain confident. He walked up to Mrs Tam with a nervous mind. She had a lifeless face when it came to Jay. With a gulp, Jay received his paper. A "*B-*" was written in red ink at the top of the paper. Next to it was written "80" and circled in the same red pen.

'Well done, Jay Ramsay. But I am sure you can certainly do better.'

Jay was actually quite happy. A *"B-"* was not a bad grade, at least according to him.

He walked back to his seat, trying not to look at his teacher. He sat near Zen who patted him on his back.

The final bell rang and Mrs. Tam departed.

Jay walked to the gate, seeing Gita along with his friend.

Zen put an arm around Jay's shoulder. 'So….not a bad day, right?'

Jay didn't have the energy to reply. He was tired.

'C'mon man! A B- is not bad! Well….much better than a C.' Zen showed his exam paper. 'So who's coming for open day?

Zen immediately realised he shouldn't have asked that.

'Are you trying to make me feel sad?' asked Jay.

'I…' A Guilt-Bomb dropped into Zen's heart. 'I-I am sorry, Jay. I forgot for a moment there.'

Jay's expression changed. He understood it was an honest mistake. Zen was not a boy who would ask such questions deliberately. He was innocent. Anyway, Zen had lost his dad as well, so he knew how Jay felt.

'Uhh….It's okay…I am just quite tired and down.'

'I understand,' replied Zen. 'You just really wish she was here.'

Jay nodded.

'Same about my dad.'

Jay looked at him. 'Well, you do have a brother,' he said. 'Me.'

Zen smiled. They had a lot of similarities in their life. It was as if they were brothers. They both had a tough childhood. They walked to the gate as Jay spotted Gita. Just after a few seconds, Zen's mom arrived in their old minivan.

'Bye dude,' he said to Jay as he ran to his mom.

Almost every single student in the school had left, except a few staying for extra classes and detention. Jay and Gita started sharing stuff about their own school days, though it was mostly Gita talking. After she went on talking for ten minutes, they realised Bingo wasn't here yet. Finally, the similar 'vroom!' of the Honda Civic was heard as Bingo pulled up near the curb.

'What happened, dad?' asked Gita.

Bingo got out of the car, pulling down his crumpled shirt.

'Sorry, for the delay. Disaster at the office.'

Jay and Gita had gotten pretty used to hearing that from Bingo.

Jay just slumped and got into the car as if he was lifeless. Gita knew how he felt and decided to leave him alone and change the subject.

'Dad, we have Open day today,' said Gita.

'What?' asked Bingo. 'When should I go?'

'At 6.'

'Oh No,' said Bingo. 'I am really sorry....I have to go to the lab at 5.'

Jay didn't know whether he had to be furious or happy.

Once they reached their house, Jay immediately went and locked himself in his room. All he needed was some alone-time.

Meanwhile, Bingo had a look at Gita's biology paper, and complimented her. He called Jay's name. There wasn't a response. It sounded like Jay wasn't at home. Gita went up to Jay's room, knocking the door. She called Jay softly but no response as usual. Gita turned back and shook her head. 'No response.'

Bingo got up from his couch and walked to the door. He gently put his ear on the wood and called, 'Jay?' This time, it was softer than the last time.

'I'm not coming out,' was the feeble reply from Jay.

Gita told Bingo about Jay's behaviour in school. She also mentioned what had happened regarding the open day. It was Jay, lonely lying on his cot. He had thrown his bag on a plastic chair, and a few books had fallen down. All the things in his room looked gruffy and were messed up. His bed wasn't arranged and blankets and pillows were lying unorganised. A pack of playing cards were lying on the floor. A black bean bag rested on the corner of his room. His face remained expressionless. Not only the average mark but the snarky comments by the bullies haunted his mind. And on mother's day….it was too much to digest for Jay. He was tightly holding his only framed photo of his mother standing in front of the *Eiffel Tower* which he always had on his round table, near his alarm clock. It was one of the few pictures Bingo had of Asha. There were crumpled, torn, newspaper clippings which had news and information related to the sightings of Stoming. The only thing which was well kept and organised was Frencher's sword, which he had got last year, leaning towards the wooden frame of the bed. It still hadn't lost its special shine. He spent some valuable time cleaning and polishing it. The cries of Bingo were barely heard by him.

'Jay!' Bingo called again.

Jay decided to show his face to Bingo and Gita, as he didn't want them to be worried. He straightened the answer sheet and added it to his file. He went to the bathroom and freshened up his face to hide the fact that he was shedding a few tears. He took a deep breath and opened the door. He saw Gita and Bingo staring at him.

'What-' Bingo was about to ask Jay, when he went into his room and shut the door once again. By now, Cookie and Poly had come into the scene as well. But, Bingo and Gita decided to let Jay console himself.

A couple of minutes passed. Jay decided to come outside. When the sound of the door was heard, everyone became quiet. Jay looked a lot better, and crashed onto the couch in the centre of the hall.

'What happened? Why's everything quiet?' he asked, sipping in some hot ginger tea from his mug.

'I think we should be the one asking that,' replied Bingo.

Jay took another sip from the ginger tea. 'It was the exam ... made me quite disappointed.'

Gita took a seat adjacent to Jay. 'I seriously don't think you would cry for that. Besides, it's a decent mark.'

But Bingo and Gita understood. It was just one of those days. Those days which makes them feel quite dejected about Asha. Thunder's cruelty and the plight of their family just made them feel a mixture of emotions which was difficult to explain. Bingo went to organise his bag for his shift at the lab at five.

Gita simply patted his back. 'Come on, let's discuss our homework with dad before he goes off to the lab. That ought to be fun.'

Jay smiled. Even though he didn't have his mom with him, he was still blessed with an amazing family.

~CHAPTER TWO~

Attacks At The Peak

It was Friday morning. Jay and the others were back to normal. The regular routine started in the morning for everyone and went on quite smoothly as well.

***

Bingo opened the door to the empty house at 1 o'clock in the afternoon. Due to a typical Friday half day at the lab, Bingo was home early. After a quick lunch, he crashed on the couch. He looked around for something to do when he saw a bunch of newspapers lying on the coffee table. He took one, putting the others back into the table. He slowly started glancing at the last page, as he never had the habit of starting from the first. There was no interesting news seen to Bingo's eyes, which made him keep it back.

He sighed. 'Boring.'

He threw the paper straight on the table. All the papers started flying in the air, and Bingo bent down to arrange them properly. He aligned all the sheets one by one, when he came to the last sheet. He was quite surprised to see the headline,

"KIDNAPPED"

A family in Chicago, consisting of six people which includes a father, an older girl and boy and three much younger children. Professional investigators claim that there was no trace of blood, except a few fingerprints and footsteps. This

leaves the family unharmed. The incident had happened today at around three a.m, though the news had leaked out only after three hours. The neighbour of the missing family, Mrs.Sleevey of fifty-seven years claimed that she heard the sound of a sudden crash, though she says that she heard nothing more.

'The Struperts were a wonderful family. Today at around four, there was a loud thud. I expected that it was some construction work and ignored it but then I heard a scream as well. After that, everything became silent,' was the observation from the scared neighbour. Though the FBI tried hard to ask questions, Mrs.Sleevey was frightened to answer more, still shaken up by last night.

-Dale Flemingster

Bingo read the article, though he felt it was just a normal kidnapping case, nothing more than that. But, he couldn't still believe what the thud was. As he kept thinking about this, he slowly dozed off on the sofa. A few hours later, Bingo stared at the clock and figured it was time for Gita and Jay's dispersal. Poly hooted and Cookie barked to stress on the point. Bingo took his sweater and car keys as he headed out to pick Jay and Gita up.

*

Thunder was happy with the recent events by his servant Ellio.

'Where should we keep him master?' he asked Thunder.

Thunder stepped down his throne and walked to Ellio who knelt down immediately, gripping the handle of his sword.

Ellio didn't move, which would be a disrespect to his master.

Thunder touched the shoulder of Ellio twice which indicated that he should stand up. He obeyed and stood upright.

'You've been good,' said Thunder, laying both his hands on Ellio's shoulders. 'I want to present a gift to you.'

He started chanting a mantra in his mind. He increased the speed gradually. A few seconds passed, and golden particles of dust started to appear. Around each particle, there was a beam of light surrounding it. More particles were starting to get generated and it started to combine. Slowly, the particles formed the shape of a sword. Finally, when all the dust particles were combined, it formed a sword. It looked similar to the Frencher's sword, though the width of the blade varied. The blade's width was narrowing from the handle, leaving itself a sharp edge. The handle had a tight grip, and had a diamond at the end. The sword was formed. Ellio lifted his hands and the swords started moving towards them leisurely. Finally, it rested on his hands. The light around the blade of the sword had vanished and it rested on Ellio's hands. Ellio's eyes dilated in amazement. It was the *Sword of Combatant.* Thunder had won several swords in his lifetime, though this was a special one. It was the third most prestigious sword in Olympia with Frencher's sword at the first, and the sword *Victrious,* which Thunder was currently using, after his Scepter vanished.

'Thank you master,' thanked Ellio. 'I shall solemnly swear that I shall use it wisely.'

'Use it well,' replied Thunder.

'About the prisoner?'

'Our brother, Stoming, is not a normal prisoner. Throw him in dungeons and have the best of guards.'

***

Gita and Jay were back from school, and Bingo wanted to share the peculiar news which he just came through. Though he shared it, Gita and Jay didn't seem so interested and just thought it was a normal kidnapping. After a fairly normal evening, the family ate dinner and dozed off.

The Saturday morning light came through the windows and glistened on the furniture. It was also the day when Ramesh had to go to Europe for a business trip and the cousins were staying at their house until Ramesh came back. A normal Saturday passed into the night. The bright full moon was visible in the sky as the bell rang. The cousins entered and said that their mom would come in a few minutes. After a few joyful skips and hops, the cousins slumped on the couch, waiting for the dinner to arrive. Tara had grown slim and was wearing double pony-tails on her hair. She was wearing a skirt with a few nice embroideries. She had a black bow on her head. Sara let her hair loose with a headband on top and wore a red and black, chequered t-shirt with grey jeans. Arjun wore a sky blue t-shirt with a gleaming Adidas logo in the middle. The bell rang again. This time, it was Riha. She looked quite dressed up, with an extreme smell of a lavender. She was wearing dark blue, rectangular spectacles and had pitch-black silky hair. Her eyebrows were quite thin, and was wearing a watch. Her lipstick was moderate and neat. She had polished her nails light pink, and wore grey jeans. Tara still looked like she was splitting her image of her. She shook hands with Bingo, and entered the room.

'Hi!' said Bingo, in a propitious manner, and welcomed her with good grace. Cookie ran from his place towards Arjun and Tara, and almost jumped on them. The slimy, wet licks were felt on the cousins' hands. He had grown a lot and developed more fur. After a good welcome, Riha also joined the wait on the couch, chatting about her work to Bingo. Due to the constant excited barks by Cookie, Bingo gave him a chew toy to play with and continued to speak with Riha. Jay and Gita were praying, as every time the cousins came there with Riha, they were with a plan of living here for at least three months. Polskite was in Gita's room as Riha still didn't know about Olympia. Everyone had settled in their places.

Bingo looked at the slightly questionable face of Riha. 'What happened? Why the nervous face?'

Riha cleared her throat. 'Actually, I was supposed to go touring with my colleagues. I haven't seen them for around over a decade but-'

'And…you want to leave them here,' finished Bingo, predicting the words of Riha.

'Yes…' said Riha. 'Look, I am really sorry but it will just be for two weeks.'

'Sure, no problem,' said Bingo. 'We like them here.'

Jay and Gita sighed in their minds but they knew they had no choice. Still, they had gotten used to them and their cousins themselves had gotten more mature.

'Sure,' said Jay.

'We'd love to have them here,' added Gita.

'Then, it's a done deal,' replied Riha.

'Where are you going?' asked Bingo.

'Munnar, Darjeeling and Gangtok back in India.'

Gita looked at Jay. 'Looks like she already booked tickets!' she whispered.

Jay nodded. 'Then, why'd she ask anyway?'

Gita shrugged.

'Where are you landing first?' asked Bingo.

'Darjeeling. The flight leaves at 6 am tomorrow.'

Riha gave a hearty good-bye to her children, Gita, Jay and Bingo as she left to her own house across the street.

Everyone went to bed after a good dinner. Bingo, who loved to sleep late on Saturdays, went to the living room and switched on the TV for some late-night entertainment. He kept scrolling the channel when he heard a loud debate. He stopped at that particular channel, and decided to watch it. He was aghast. A house was telecasted, surrounded by police and FBI. Then, a newsreader started speaking, when a 'breaking news' symbol flashed into the screen.

'I'm Steve Houston reporting from Las Vegas. Another case. This time, it has turned worse. Six murdered in Las Vegas. Just a few miles away from the Paris hotel! People are persuaded that there's a link between the family missing at Chicago and the Las Vegas incident, while some do not. The FBI confirmed that it is a murder case, as they looked tortured, with burns all over their body. Layla Coven, John Coven, Mr. Coven, Tony Markez, Agatha Markez and Marva Markez were the people found dead. Unfortunately, that young lively batch included a bunch of children as well. The Markez folks were devastated by this news. This time, there were traces of dust particles and the floor was extremely damaged, and moreover burnt. Mrs. Coven, who was transferred to Portland for her job, was extremely dejected and crestfallen, and she claims that her husband

knew no one so dangerous, going to an extent for a murder. Has the evil A.B.A Stoming returned? He is the only one who had an ability to murder someone in such a heavily guarded city. Not one, but six!'

The reporter had finished speaking, when a plain red screen flashed up. New sentences started appearing with a man reading those instructions.

'SAFETY MEASURES TO FOLLOW FOR YOUR OWN GOOD

1. Never ever go out of your house alone.

2. If you come across any strange-looking person, immediately inform the nearest cop and don't ever try to handle it yourself.

3. If you hear the doorbell, peep in through the peephole and open it if you only see a person YOU KNOW.

4. If you hear someone shouting/ suffering from pain, shut the door and lock it immediately and call 911 to that location.

5. Any person staying alone in the house may go to their native places.

6. Avoid getting out after 7:00 p.m.

We are trying our best to detect the culprit, but YOUR SAFETY is in YOUR HANDS.'

The screen had vanished, revealing the face of the news anchor who was reading it out loud. Bingo couldn't believe what he was seeing. A family missing in Chicago, and another murdered! He knew that there was a link between the two cases in two main cities of the United States. That too, both the cases were related to families. He was worried at the same time. Then, he went to the next channel. It telecasted the same news, with more terror. The headline was *A Murder in Casino city*.

He was sure it wasn't Stoming, but who is it? Is the killer related to Olympia or Thunder? Why should he only kill families? Do the murders have anything to do with him and his family? All these questions were running in Bingo's head. He wasn't interested in listening more. He switched off the television and went to his room to sleep.

The sun had just risen. Bingo was already up and on the sofa. Gita was out and saw Bingo.

Gita smirked. 'Someone is up early.'

'You saw the newspaper?' asked Bingo.

'Nope. Why?'

'You may want to see it.'

Gita took the newspaper which was rearranged again into her hands, her face turned pale when she saw the article.

'Whoa! Six people?'

'Yep. And the strange part is that they are all families, murdered all at once.'

Just as those words popped out of Bingo's mouth, Jay entered the room in his silk pyjamas and peach-coloured slippers.

'Jay, look at this.' Bingo handed over the paper to Jay.

Jay walked towards Bingo and read the news on the first page.

His mouth opened in shock. He had seen the previous kidnapping before but this one was VERY similar to the previous one. That fact haunted him. 'Do you think Thunder has to do with this?'

Gita was still quite sceptical. 'We don't know but we think it's a regular kidnapping and murdering case.'

Jay continued reading but one point enraged him. 'How dare they accuse Stoming if they have no proof!'

'You can't blame them. They have no other work to do other than blame others,' said Bingo.

'Yeah, Stoming was in fact a cold-blooded killer,' agreed Gita. 'He has changed now though, I hope.'

Bingo brushed off the topic. 'Let us leave that matter for the day. After all, you have a glorious day to spend with the cousins.'

Jay and Gita groaned.

After that, the matter was forgotten. The cousins woke up as the bell rang. It was Riha, to wish a final good-bye before her trip.

Riha looked like she was in a rush but her dress and her make-up was quite fine. She was talking to someone as she tried hugging her children at the same time.

Riha was shouting into the phone. 'Hello! I can't hear you!'

Tara giggled. 'Mom, you have kept the phone upside down!'

'Oh.' She turned the phone back upright as she threw a water bottle to Jay who caught it with a bit of a struggle.

'Hold on one moment please.' Riha turned to her children and gave a kiss on the cheek to each of them and she put her phone back in her purse after speaking a few more words to her caller.

Now, Bingo was listening to Riha's rules for the cousins.

'Yeah. Yeah. We know,' reassured Bingo.

'And their nap time is at-'

'9:00. We know,' finished Gita. 'Gee. Take it easy. We've done this two times before.'

'I know. I am just stressed out. The flight will leave a little early today.'

Sara pointed her finger at her mom's face. 'Mom, you have something on your face.'

In response, Riha took a tissue and wiped her face where Sara was pointing at. She felt a sticky substance on her cheek. When she wiped it, she saw a red hue on the tissue paper. 'Thanks, dear.'

Riha grabbed her bottle from Jay and waved a hearty good-bye to her children. Her phone rang once again as she left the house. Bingo closed the door for her. He peeped out the window to see Riha loading her suitcases in a taxi and leaving in the car.

Jay had to get to his school, even though it was a Sunday, to pick up one of the mechanical parts of his robot which he had forgotten in his school lab. His lab teacher had assigned him robotics homework, which was one of the rare homework he was excited about. He had called the school the day before and the janitor had told a suitable time to pick it up from the lost and found box. He dressed up casually and decided to ride his bike to school. His bike was quite cool and attractive looking, with a few racing designs. He wanted to get his item as soon as possible after he glimpsed the dark, grey clouds in the sky. The roads were all empty, and didn't have a lot of vehicles except a car or two. He was halfway through, when he wiped off a raindrop. Finally, he reached the school. He was appalled. A huge wall in the school had shattered, on which the giant board, which had the name of the school, had fallen. The debris filled the entire plot of land on which the school was on. There were police vehicles parked all around, with the blaring sound of sirens filling the air. He couldn't walk any more as a dew-filled caution tape had been put. A crew of fire-fighters made their dramatic entrance and parked next to the police vehicles. The press was getting every bit of this commotion on camera and they interviewed a few people as well.

One media person came sprinting towards Jay. 'Are you a student in this school?'

'Y-yes,' replied Jay, not recovered from the shock of his school being shattered.

A few cameras flashed around Jay as the reporter put the mike closer to his mouth. 'How does it feel that your beloved school was half destroyed?'

'I honestly don't know how this happened. I had just come here to retrieve something. I didn't expect this.'

The camera man took one last flash of Jay's shocked face and ran off with his reporter to capture the fire-fighters and police in action.

Second by second, more vehicles started arriving and more folks gathered around. After a few minutes, the principal walked out along with a few guards around him. Random questions shot out as the principal and his guards pushed through the crowd, answering one or two questions here and there. Along with the mix of the sirens, the whole place was extremely ear-piercing and was blasting with tension and curiosity. Then, he saw a fat plump police officer walking to the press, saying that there were no students, as the incident had happened at night.

Jay immediately got on his bike and started towards his house. He started pedalling as fast as he could until he reached the familiar looking two-storey building. He parked his bike next to Gita's bike and Bingo's car. He raced into the house and slammed the door behind him.

Bingo heard the noise and ran towards the front door. He saw Jay, holding his knees and panting.

'The school….it's destroyed,' said Jay, slowly catching his breath. 'Another attack.'

Gita too came to check all the commotion with the cousins as Bingo switched on the television. The first photo he could see was the picture of the school, with almost one half of it destroyed. Jay's image appeared on the TV as he answered the questions asked by the reporter.

Bingo looked at Jay and smirked.

'What?' asked Jay. 'They came and asked me!'

Tara's face brightened up as she saw Jay's face on the TV. 'Hey! You're on the news!' But once she saw the condition of her school, her smile turned into a frown. 'Oh.'

Now, the family was sure that it was done by Thunder or someone under his rule. It was night again after another gloomy day. Gita and Jay had trouble sleeping, whereas the cousins slept soundly. Bingo had seen a movie in the night again. The clock kept ticking and it was midnight. Another hour passed and it was 1:30 a.m. Bingo was lying on his bed with the faint sound of Arjun snoring next to him. Suddenly a thump sound was heard. Cookie and Arjun immediately woke up and Bingo's feet found the ground. Cookie started barking continuously. It was heard again. This time, it was louder. Now, along with the sound of someone panting. There was a dark shadow outside the window. It grew in size and became taller. Apart from the growls, Cookie's barking was the only sound heard. The others had woken up by now after hearing the sounds. Everyone heard Cookie barking and went near him. Cookie led the half-sleepy, half-terrified bunch down the stairs, to the living room and to the front door. Jay had taken his sword on the way and was ready to strike. Bingo signalled Cookie to stop barking and hesitantly walked towards the front door. He also signalled the others to stay behind him. He slowly peeped through the peephole. The memories of the murder cases haunted him as he was rethinking his decision. There were two shadowy figures seen through the peephole, one large, one a bit slim but tall. Their features weren't clear due to the pitch dark midnight sky.

Suddenly, the doorbell rang.

The cousins' breath was almost knocked out due to the sudden sound of the doorbell. 'AHHHHHHH!!!' they screamed.

This made the others panic-stricken too. Gita reached out to the handle and was about to open it, when Jay was preparing for a powerful slash. Bingo tried shutting the cousins and he succeeded too. Everything was quiet as everyone's heartbeats thumped ferociously.

Gita looked at the others. 'Ready?'

Jay nodded.

She opened it and immediately closed her eyes. Jay was about to slash the second Gita opened the door. But when he saw who was outside, he immediately aborted his strike. There were two people, a middle-aged man, and a teen-age girl. The man was wearing a thick, blue sweater and regular jeans. He looked bulk and gave an impression of a wrestler. He also had a belt with a quiver of arrows and a bow and an iron dagger. It also had a glowing blue sphere, next to the sword. The girl had blonde hair, looked slim, and had a similar sweater to Az, only hers was a bit thicker and had more embroideries and designs. Apart from the usual sword in her scabbard, she was holding a thick book, looking as if it had eight hundred pages. She didn't wear a hood or any type of mask, and her face was well seen which made Jay recognize who it was. Az and Partha.

'May we come in for a sip of hot chocolate?' asked Partha, teasingly.

Az smiled. 'Some strong Coffee as well.

~CHAPTER THREE~

Again?

Jay lowered his sword and clearly saw the faces of Partha and Az entering the house. He was clearly surprised, as he didn't expect to see his friends to come and visit him. Not only him, but everyone breathed a sigh of relief. They both entered the house. All the lights weren't even switched on in the excitement. Az and Partha sat down on the couch. They looked quite fine but a hint of tiredness was seen upon their faces. Gita and Bingo immediately went to the kitchen, to prepare some coffee and hot chocolate. After a bit of catching up, Gita and Bingo came back with the steaming hot coffee for Az and the hot chocolate for Partha. Cookie was quite shaken by the recent events and was continuously sniffing Partha and Az's legs as if they were imposters.

Partha looked up from her hot chocolate mug. 'Tell your dog to stay away. I am not a threat.'

Cookie immediately backed off and sat on the sofa next to Jay who petted him comfortingly.

Az gulped the hot coffee and put it on the coffee table in front of him. He wiped off some coffee drops from his mouth. 'I'm feelin' much better.'

'Well, that was a very kind welcome,' said Partha, taking another sip of her hot chocolate.

She had changed a lot from four months ago. Her attitude was much sterner and she also wanted everything to be perfect. Az too, was much more casual than they'd ever seen. He didn't look worried one bit.

'So...why are you all here?' asked Jay, stroking Cookie's soft fur.

Partha put her hot chocolate mug down on the table. 'Oh right,' she said. 'We wanted to warn you about the dangers that might happen.'

'You mean Thunder-related?'

Partha nodded.

'Whatever happens, I'm not ready to come back to that bloody planet with my family again,' said Bingo.

'No, I mean in your world,' said Az.

'Here?' asked Bingo. 'You mean the recent attacks?'

'Yeah.'

'They were quite similar…'

'Thunder is targeting your family,' chimed Partha.

Bingo, Gita and Jay had understood the coincidental information in all those kidnappings. The families were quite similar to theirs.

Suddenly, Bingo's mobile phone vibrated a little and made a notification sound. Bingo, hearing that sound, took the phone out of his pocket. He picked up the phone and there was a new notification that popped out.

'*1 new message from Oak Hills School.*'

He quickly clicked the notification, typed in the password as it took Bingo to the messages column where a shocking, yet expected message was given.

Sara peeped over to Bingo's phone. 'What did they post?'

Bingo lent the phone to everyone to see.

'Dear students, I regret to say that the schools were damaged due to a shocking attack. Don't worry, we've reported the issue to the police to keep you all safe. The schools shall be repaired by a month's time. The topics have been taught thoroughly and homework will be sent online. We expect the students to study the topics for quizzes which will be given by the end of the leave. We highly recommend the students to not consider this as a break and put their efforts for the upcoming tests. STAY HOME STAY SAFE.'

-Principal Henry Catane of Oak Hills Middle and High School and Principal Becky Clayton of Oak Hills Elementary School

As Jay was reading, Partha also peeked into the phone to see what was going on.

The message had proved her point. 'So, this is what I was warning you about. Thunder had planned more attacks in other parts of the country. Looks like he skipped directly to your school.'

'Thunder, as he didn't know your exact location, destroyed all the families that were similar in number and age to yours. He started attacking a few but then found the location of your school and figured you'd be inside, sleeping. But unfortunately he didn't know how the schools work here and destroyed an empty school. But if we leave you for the night, you are dead. Thunder probably knows where your house is by now.'

'Then how did he know where to get us when we were babies?' asked Gita.

'I think he let Stoming do that part.'

Jay took Cookie in his lap. 'Speaking of Stoming, where is he?'

Partha's face turned expressionless. She was silent for a few seconds but finally found her words. 'Actually, he went into the castle to retrieve mom…'

Jay already wasn't liking where this was going.

'And he….kind of got captured.'

Jay's mouth opened in shock. 'What?'

Gita almost pinched herself. 'How? He knows each and every thing about Thunder and his guards!'

Partha shrugged. 'I don't know. We devised a plan to break in and find out about mom. The plan didn't go quite well though as Thunder had set a trap for Stoming.'

All that was going through Jay's mind was Partha's voice saying that Stoming was captured. *Stoming is captured, Stoming is captured*, and it rang like a bell. He couldn't believe it.

'So, is Thunder planning to ransom him or something?' asked Bingo.

Az scoffed in a mocking way. 'You think Thunder's so kind-hearted? If he has the chance, he'll kill him then and there but he generally chooses torture.'

Jay gulped a huge taste of bitterness in his mouth. 'No, we can't let Stoming die! We have to save him no matter what.'

'Whoa, whoa, whoa. Hold on there, kid,' said Az. 'There are more matters we need to worry about.'

'We can put them aside for a couple of days. But first we need to save Stoming.'

'I'm afraid there's a bigger problem than that.'

'Why are you not worrying about him, you idiot?' Jay was getting impatient. All his mind told was to save Stoming no matter the consequences. 'He's your friend!'

Az was taken aback, but still found his words. 'I'm afraid if we don't do this, Thunder might kill Stoming.'

Jay stopped as he was going to shoot out an argument. He turned a bit calmer. 'But won't it be simpler to just save him and get out of there?'

'If Stoming got captured, who's to say that we won't? Thunder might be expecting us to come to him.'

Jay decided against his usual revenge plan and decided to listen and consider Az's option.

'Yeah so you remember that there are five 'Enchanted Books' right?'

'Yeah,' said Gita. 'Who could forget?'

'Okay. So, we have to find and retrieve the third book, *The Enchanted Book Of Resurrection* before Thunder does.'

'How will it kill Stoming if we don't complete this task?' Gita asked.

'Thunder can't actually kill his own brother, be it a half-brother or a flesh-and-blood brother. It is against the ancient rules of Olympia. So, if he gets the book, he can have an opposing force. He can kill Stoming and bring back someone else using the book.'

Gita scoffed. 'Since when does Thunder care about rules?'

Az chuckled. 'He doesn't. The breaking of these rules can result in harsh punishment, even death, so I don't think Thunder will risk it.'

'Why don't Thunder's men just kill Stoming instead of Thunder himself?' asked Bingo.

'Not that easy. He is much more powerful than the others. He can only die when someone attacks him out of the blue. That won't happen due to the security of Thunder's prison. Even Thunder's minions aren't allowed near it. Only special, trustworthy sorcerers are called to guard it.'

'Okay…' said Bingo. 'Do you know where to find the book at least?'

'We do,' replied Partha. She started flipping through the book which she carried. It had a brown cover, and had the title, *Frencher: The Killer Of Sinners.*

She continued flipping and glimpsed at the words on a few pages to check if it was the page she was looking for. Towards the end of the 800 paged book, a blank page with two handwritten sentences was seen. Partha stopped at that page. The words were written using black ink. Partha lifted the book and showed it straight to Gita's and Jay's face.

"The place where dark souls roam,

In the other part of the dome." was written in the black ink.

'Other part of the dome?' asked Gita. 'You mean the west?'

Partha didn't bother to even give a nod and flipped to the sixty-ninth chapter of the book, with the title,

"Dangerous Sites and Prophecies Of Olympia"

And stopped by the six hundred and seventy second page. Partha looked for the particular line and finally came by it. She read,

'The Land Of The Phantoms. The place where the darkest of souls reside, is still said to be haunted. The Land Of The Phantoms is also known as the 'Living Graveyard'. It is a home to the darkest creatures such as the Vulture Of

Flames, Ostragons and some very spine-chilling places such as the graveyard of lost toys. This place has the Fego River which spits out venomous fire. This fire cannot be extinguished. This land has skeletons lying on the floor which move at the sight of any other soul entering. This area is said to be a very mysterious place with red smoke all around. Olympers believes that The Land Of The Phantoms used to be a beautiful place with mega butterflies bustling around in joy. This area had the most beautiful creatures in the world. It was the home of the magical rabkeys. Rabkeys were very powerful and joyful creatures. It is said that some sorcerers got their power from rabkeys. The Dondelious' Empire was once here. Even though the gnomes lived in their own kingdom, they spent more time here than in their own kingdom. King Dondelious the fifth was a very nice king and would arrange fabulous events and functions in the outskirts. His castle was a few miles away from the border of Flogreya which was what it was called back then. The gnomes would just visit the castle just for a sight of their adjacent land which the king didn't mind. The gnomes' kingdom was very organised and would not allow the people to venture into Flogreya and would arrange a specific time to do so.

One day, there was a major war between Dondelious' kingdom and the gnome king of Jysterd, a planet very far away from Olympia, the home of Thunder's bloodline. Unlike Thunder's war with Frencher, Dondelious and his army were victorious. People cheered and yelled triumphantly 'ALL HAIL DONDELIOUS!' as he gave a last strike of his sword towards their leader. For the gnomes, when the leader was defeated, all of them had to retreat. Even if he's vanquished in less than a minute. When all the people vanished in retreat, the gnome started clapping hands and cheering as Dondelious lifted his sword up in the air as it caught light. Unfortunately, this war caused a lot of damage to Flogreya which was basically a wasteland after it. The king of Olympia at that time was none other than Frencher's grandfather, Koasfert. Koasfert was an evil wicked man and never liked the gnomes or Flogreya. He was pretty shocked later when he saw that his grandson (Frencher) loved sharing and was loved by a lot of people. That day, Koasfert was walking near the gnomes' kingdom plotting his punishment for a misdeed by his servant when he heard the cheering noise of the gnomes. He strolled towards the gnome kingdom and peeped over from a bush. He saw the gnomes cheering triumphantly with Flogreya withering around them. 'Ha!' he thought. This is the perfect excuse!

He slowly levitated across some grass and landed in the battlefield of the gnomes. The gnomes were shocked to see his presence. He looked around, pretending to be appalled and agitated.

'Oh no!' He shouted with his hands over his heart. 'What happened? Gnomes, is this your doing?'

'What are you talking about?' asked Dondelious.

He and his people also wore magicheds (little ear buds) to protect them from the voice of Koasfert. 'And most importantly, why are you here?'

'You do know not to speak to your king like that.'

'You're not our king.'

'That's not very nice...but anyway what happened to this beautiful land? Did you party all night and destroy it?'

Dondelious was taken aback by that sentence. 'Us? Never! We love this land! You hate it!'

'And why should I believe you?'

'Well, because I have hundreds of inscriptions in our library to prove your evilness,' replied a surprisingly calm Dondelious.

'That's it! I've had it with your shenanigans!' shouted the evil Koasfert. 'From today, I shall curse you. This land will turn into a living nightmare with the

darkest of creatures in this realm. They all shall roam here. This place should not be approachable to anybody and shall have spine-chilling illusions. No matter how much I love this land, sacrifices have to be made.'

The gnomes were shocked at Koasfert's curse. Dondelious was infuriated at this unfairness.

'No!' he shouted, not accepting the curse. Koasfert didn't reply and with one swift flick of his finger Dondelious' head was sliced off his body. The gnomes were scared at this horrible sight and ran away back to their kingdom, whimpering. From then the beautiful Flogreya became Phatavir and then later on became The Land Of Phantoms much later after the Enchanted Books were formed.

'Okay…' replied Gita, taking her eyes off the book. She rubbed her eyes a bit due to the small font. 'What is the point of this?'

'That's where the book is. That's where we should go,' said Az.

The family was left with no clue. Bingo wasn't quite ready for his family to take another risk of his family being killed. His mind was filled with the ghosts of his past.

'There should be someone guarding, right?' asked Jay.

Partha immediately flipped a few pages until they saw the chapter title - "The Guardian Of Resurrection".

But even with the big build up, there wasn't any information about who it was. So they had no idea. It could be anybody - from a blood-curling monster to a witty old man.

Jay understood the risks of this plan but the life of Stoming's life was too much of a chance to take. 'We are going.'

'You're kidding, aren't you?' replied Bingo. He had been in this situation before but the risks only appealed to him.

'Dad. Stoming can't die. He just can't.'

'I can say the same thing about you, Jay.'

Gita nodded in agreement.

Luckily, Jay had a good comeback. 'Look, we've done this before. And I don't think these things are going to stop happening. We were chosen to find these books. And I know I might sound like I'm bragging but we have no choice. If we stay here, we are dead. You know that.'

It did not take long to convince Gita and Bingo. They were quite impressed.

Gita patted Jay's shoulder. 'Wow! I think you should join the debate club.'

Jay shook his head. 'Nah, too much work.'

Gita sighed. She expected such an answer.

'When are we leaving?' asked Bingo, still questioning his own decision.

'At the birth of dawn,' replied Partha.

Gita became more alert. 'Then we need to start packing, ASAP.'

She started running to the room along with Bingo when Partha stood her and pulled her back. 'No need to pack, miss.'

'Why?' asked Gita. 'And don't call me "miss". 'Gita' would do just fine.'

Partha ignored her appeal. 'The only advantage of the Land Of Phantoms is that you won't starve from hunger. Perhaps, you won't feel it at all. Mostly because you won't notice it after seeing all those creatures. A gram of food in your stomach would sustain you for a month.'

Bingo's face was still sceptical. He had faced many hardships related to Thunder and Olympia and didn't like thinking about it. His wife had died, he had almost died, and his son had almost died as well. Not what you call "happy memories". Whatever the others said was a glitch in his ears. The thought of Olympia's troubles haunted him. But Bingo agreed with Jay's point. They had no choice. No matter what they do, Olympia's troubles will be at their tail, ready to pounce. 'Well, then, let's go back to sleep. We need our rest for this adventure.'

~CHAPTER FOUR~

A Swampy Start

Everyone agreed with Bingo's suggestion and hit the sack in less than two minutes. Even with his regained confidence, his sleep was still delayed by a bit. He couldn't help staring out of his window and looking out at the stars for a few minutes to soak the situation in. He happened to see a shooting star and he had one universal wish. 'Please protect my children at all cost.'

***

It was eight in the morning. Even though the sun was already supposed to be up, the sky was cloudy and overcast. Partha, as an early riser, similar to Gita who woke up much earlier at six when the sun hadn't even risen up. Az was an early riser too. Jay had got up, and started polishing the blade of his sword, making it very lustrous, and the cousins gulped a glass of chocolate milk into their languid throats. No one had got up, except a few newspaper boys racing through the streets on their bikes. The sky was overcast so the morning sunlight didn't fall through the windows of many houses. Instead it remained a dull morning with puffy grey clouds covering the sky. Partha started arranging her arrows into her quiver, and tightened the string of the bow. She was showing Gita how to maintain her bow neatly. Gita followed these steps. Jay started reading the newspaper looking for headlines that might be a clue of Thunder's servants' recent whereabouts. Fortunately he found no recent murder or kidnapping case. He breathed a sigh of relief. Bingo had just woken up and was brushing his teeth. He was feeling a little less worried now and was calm. Az was just sipping black coffee on the dining table when Gita came into the room.

'We don't have all day!' indicated Az, pointing at his hand as though there was a watch there. 'Thunder's servants could attack us any minute now!' Everyone paused their work and got up. Cookie gave a serious expression and Poly bent her head forward and hooted. She was a different type of owl. An owl that is not nocturnal. Probably because she is originally a griffin. Az gathered everybody around. Everybody went outside of the house in the slightly nippy air. A cool wind was blowing with an overcast sky. Outside of their house, there was a small device attached to the door near the label saying, 'DR RAMSAY'S RESIDENCE' which stood in the centre of the door and was printed in bold letters. Az had a small spherical device in his hand. It was a crystal ball which looked pretty similar to the ball in Thunder's scepter. Az placed the device on the outside wall of the house, near the door. The ball seemed to stick to the wall. Then, Az touched the ball with his other hand. When he did so, the device started expanding rapidly. It became a bigger crystal ball and then it sprouted hand-like crystal materials from it. It was a marvellous sight. Slowly it sprouted ten legs and the crystal ball remained in the middle. Az put his hand over it and it started lighting up as if it was sensing where Az wanted to go. 'Come on everyone!'

Everyone scurried towards Az and started joining their hands like a chain, along with all their bows and arrows in their quivers and swords and daggers in their scabbards. Poly glided down and perched on the shoulder of Jay and Cookie stood beside Gita, holding her sweatpants with his teeth. Az wanted to confirm if all were ready, as there was no chance of returning back home.

'It takes three seconds to go there, but there are chances to take eternity to come back,' without giving anyone to really think about what he said, he shouted, 'In three, two and one!' He paused for a moment to look at everybody. 'Let's go!'

The crystal ball in the teleporter spun with all its force. So did the family. Grey smoke appeared around them. They all shouted helplessly while Partha and Az were expressionless as they were used to it. Poly hooted loudly. It was a total madhouse. They all held to each other as tightly as possible for dear life. Suddenly the environment changed around them. Instead of an overcast sky, there came an orange sky. Instead of a grassy land they had slammed onto a filthy and slushy floor, filled with wet soil and puddles.

'That was a rough ride,' said Jay, getting up and loosening his limbs, which was followed by everyone. The cousins slowly got up, brushing off the dirt, and noticed that they had crashed onto a swamp, full of dirt and slush. Partha stood up, not showing any pain on her face and cleaned her elbows. They started searching for Bingo, and didn't know where he was as usual.

Az barely flicked a piece of slush from his arm He put the crystal teleporter in his pocket and looked at everyone else, who were removing slush from their clothes vigorously. 'Hope everyone's here and fine.'

Jay pointed at a tree. 'I...don't think so.'

In the tree was Bingo, as usual, hanging up-side-down, clinging to the branch of the tree, which looked like it was going to fall any moment.

'What do you think you are doing there Mr. Ramsay?' asked Partha, looking at the unusual posture of Bingo. Bingo was scared looking down.

'HELP!' His face looked like there was the largest herd of wild buffaloes running towards him at full speed. Everyone ran towards the poor man, and noticed that the branch was gradually cracking, not able to bear the weight of Bingo. His glasses dropped down into a puddle, which gave a clear sample of what was going to happen to him.

The tree was not as tall as the trees they saw the last time, though it was reasonable.

'WHY IS IT ALWAYS ME?' shouted Bingo, still clinging on. The crack was expanding continuously, and a fall from that height would at least cost a couple of limbs.

'Exactly what are we supposed to do?' Partha asked Jay.

'As if I know!' replied Jay. 'Dad! Hold on! I'm thinking!'

'Before you finish your thinking I will reach heaven!' replied Bingo. The branch was about to break any second now.

Bingo had no choice but to tightly close his eyes, and pray to the lord. Looking down made him more scared and created more panic. Finally, the branch was not able to handle the weight and snapped in half. Unfortunately, Bingo was holding the broken half. The family barely had time to shout before they saw a flash before their eyes as it looked like Bingo was plucked from thin air. But their relief was quick as they heard Bingo's voice. 'Ho Ho! Thanks my friend!' They looked towards their right. It was Polskite! Not Poly the owl, it was the real Polskite, the griffin! Polskite soared up into the sky, and Bingo was enjoying himself. The family appeared as dots to him. He could see the giant lake, the river of poison, everything, covered by a huge umbrella of fresh, lush green trees with light showering his body. Polskite decided to get back, and glided down. Bingo had just experienced a brief, sky tour of the great Olympia, and the unbelievable beauties of it. Polskite landed down, running at lightning speed like a landed jet running on the runway.

Finally, she slowed down. Bingo jumped down from the loyal griffin and patted him on the shoulder comfortingly. The family, Az and Partha were a few metres behind and he could see Gita running over to him.

'Ya feeling good?' asked Az, who was next to Gita.

'Not good. Brilliant!' replied Bingo.

'Is this really Olympia? It's extremely different!' said Jay.

'Boy, you have to understand a thing,' said Az. 'The Olympia which you saw the last time was just a tip of the iceberg. There are more places undiscovered and perhaps more dangerous. From my days, if we pass these groves, the real city appears.'

'Olympia had cities?'

'Of course they had!' joined Partha. 'It was just like a normal city.'

They noticed Polskite following them, and making grunts. They realised that he had to visit his home, and also that he would have obviously missed his pride. Bingo turned back, and gave a last stroke to Polskite who bowed, and stepped back. She started galloping as fast as a cheetah and soared up into the blue sky.

'Anyway,' said Az. 'Let's get going.

The family walked and walked as usual. Apart from the slush of the swamp, the scene around them was pretty scenic. Many tall trees were around them, rising high into the orange sky. The forest of trees were also home to many creatures who happily enjoyed the slightly swampy smell and the clear weather. Rabkeys hopped all around the banks of the swamp.

But with the scenic beauty around them, the swamp became slushier or at least, that is how it seemed to. Arjun felt the slush enter his socks. 'Yuck!' he screamed as he shook his feet frantically.

On the slush, there was a weed-like-plant, whose leaves were of the shape of hearts, and the stem navy blue. Sara bent down and plucked it, taking it towards her nose. The smell was extremely horrible, and smelled like the blend of dirty socks and garlic breath. She immediately took it away from her nose and showed it to Az.

'Uhh, what's this?' she asked.

Az got the weed from Tara and smelt it for a moment. He had a similar reaction to Sara, and immediately guessed what it was.

'Consentire,' he said. 'Has the ability to make anyone agree with whatever you are saying. The most expensive weed. Also the rarest.'

'Can I have it?' asked Sara

'Your choice,' replied Az. Just don't smell it.'

Sara checked if her jeans had a pocket and when she found it, she put it in carefully.

Slowly, debris started to fill the ground. At first, the marshy ground was dominant but the debris of broken glass and pieces of metal increased until the swamp was barely visible. A rabkey hopped into the shadow, and it seemed as if suddenly, the whole ground was like a scrap-metal-yard. There were remains of buildings which looked like they were tall once upon a time, but now they were barely the height of a dump truck. They also had uncountable cracks and broken building glasses. There were blood stains on the walls of the buildings, which added extra eeriness to the already creepy atmosphere.

Jay picked up a rusted pipe from the floor. 'I thought Olympia was a clean place but…' he scanned the scene. 'Apparently, I wasn't right.'

Partha understood what this place was. 'The abandoned city of Olympia.' She barely gave everyone any time to process this as she started running. Everyone followed her, some faster than others. Finally, she stopped.

'Where do you think you are going?' Az asked his daughter.

Partha was still muted, and pointed at a half-destroyed park. There was a broken steel gate. The grass had withered and had almost camouflaged with the dry, red soil. Some old pathways were visible as well in between the dry grass.

'Someone should go,' he replied.

'Huh?'

'Stoming. Someone should go to retrieve him.'

'Really? Now you are realising?'

Az winced. 'I know. But we have no choice. Who is with me?'

'We are.' said Sara, referring to her siblings.

Arjun was surprised. 'We are?' he asked, which was immediately followed by a sharp kick from Sara. Arjun regained his senses. 'Yeah. We are.'

'Remember, there is no internet,' mused Bingo.

Sara gave an annoyed face to Bingo. 'Ha-ha. Very funny. I am serious now. For a change.'

'Are you serious?' asked Bingo. 'It's going to be dangerous.'

'Much less dangerous than a land of ghosts. I am sure Tara would agree.' Sara pointed at Tara who shuddered in reply. 'Anyway, we have been there before. We have experience.'

'She has a point,' agreed Az. Him and everyone understood Sara's point but the thought that Sara and the cousins had volunteered by themselves still remained a shock. But Az still thought he needed more people. He looked at Bingo. 'Dr Ramsay?'

'Don't call me Dr Ramsay. Bingo is fine.'

'I need you to come along too.'

'What?' said Bingo 'No way! I need to protect my children.'

Az put a hand on Bingo's shoulder. 'Look. I understand. Partha is the only family I have. But they need to learn to fend for themselves.'

Bingo was still not approving of the idea. 'Nuh uh. These are my kids. They can't travel over a land filled with phantoms and dark creatures! Are you insane?'

'Bingo, if you help us free Stoming, he could help all of us in a great way.'

Bingo was a little convinced but not fully. He had agreed to this whole trip as long as he could stay near his children and protect them 24/7. 'They can't go by themselves! They need adult supervision!'

Jay decided to intervene. 'Dad! We are more than sixteen years old! We can take care of ourselves.'

'Yeah, dad!' supported Gita.

'Mr Ramsay, I'll make sure that I'll protect them,' said Partha.

Jay was offended. 'Hey! We can take care of ourselves!'

Gita crossed her arms. 'For the record, I am older than you.'

'See, they all are very talented. Plus Jay is the prophesied one. Believe me, I've tested his powers. Gita has amazing shooting skills and my daughter can shoot and sword fight.' asked Az

Jay and Gita were surprised. 'You can sword fight?'

'Hey! Can't a person have two talents?' Partha took out her sword. It had a polished copper blade which gleamed in the light. It had a handle made of fine dragon skin. It had a strong grip for holding and was very smooth when touched. The blade looked sharp and menacing. The sword was at least 12 inches long with a griffin feather at the end. Everybody except Az was awestruck by it. Bingo was slowly getting convinced.

'This is my most lethal weapon,' Partha said.

To give a show, she took the sword and started wielding it. Unfortunately, Jay was the victim. He didn't expect the first strike but his relatively newfound power helped him to block it.

Partha slammed and Jay blocked, this happened a lot of times.

When she reached close to Jay, she jumped with her sword in her hand. Jay tried shielding him with his sword but it was too late.

Partha struck Jay. When Jay waited for him to die and to be sent to heaven, nothing happened. When Jay looked around, he saw the same sky, the same red soil and the sight that lay in front of him didn't decrease his shock. Partha's sword was going through him like he was a hologram!

'Who are you and where is my son?' questioned Bingo. 'That's just a hologram!'

'Your son is right there,' replied Partha. 'It's another power of my sword. It recognises who is a real friend and who's not. If it's not a real friend the sword will kill him immediately. I had to test it on Jay. I had my doubts.'

'Hey!' commented Jay, still recovering from the shock.

'Nice,' commented Bingo, fully convinced. He knew that these three would be a good trio and would keep each other safe. 'Fine...I shall come with you to save Stoming.'

Az patted his shoulder. 'Good for you.' he said. 'Okay, I think we might as well part now.'

'Yeah, we might as well,' replied Bingo.

Az walked up to Partha and kissed her forehead. 'Stay safe dear.'

'You too, dad.'

Gita and Jay ran to Bingo and gave warm hugs. Bingo stood upright and his eyes looked confident.

Gita knelt down to the three cousins. 'Don't touch anything. No pranks.'

The cousins nodded in acknowledgement.

'C'mon guys!' reminded Az. 'We don't have all day!' He was good at subtle reminders like that.

Az took the teleporter out of his pocket and activated it. Bingo, the cousins and Az joined their hands.

'Three, two and ONE!' yelled Az, when they started spinning all around. After a few seconds of dizziness, they crashed onto normal sand. Az slowly opened his eyes, and gave a hand to the others.

Bingo scanned all around, and saw that there were no abandoned things, there were no swamps and puddles. Nothing was there except tall trees and plants growing on dry sand.

'Looks like we have teleported,' said Az. 'Let's do this once again.'

* * *

Now, Partha, Jay and Gita were the only ones left for the quest into the dark side of Olympia, known as The Land Of Phantoms. They had to know that they had to be safe, and always stay together, as things wouldn't be as easy as they think in the darker dome. Wicked creatures awaited them, along with a few surprises. Jay pulled out his sword, and Gita and Partha were ready.

'Do you think they went safe?' Jay asked everyone.

'Didn't look like it,' said Gita. 'But they should have.'

'From now, dangers may shoot out anytime they want. We should have a plan.'

'And good that I carried a picnic box of food just in case,' said Gita. 'They won't starve out there I guess.'

They started convoying towards the end of the great scrap-metal-yard. When Jay was walking, he noticed something on the floor. He immediately stopped in his tracks to pick it up. Partha and Gita noticed that Jay had stopped and turned back to seek the reason. They saw Jay picking up a rectangular piece of parchment clinging on a plastic lid. It wasn't crumpled at all, but quite folded unnecessarily on the corners. When Jay picked it up, Gita and Partha peeked over at the parchment. Jay finally looked at the paper and was dismayed. It was a plain piece of paper. He waited for a couple of seconds, hoping for something to happen and so did the others. And so it did. Slowly, pictures started appearing on it, along with its colour. It was a map! It contained pictures of landforms, exactly how it looked. First appeared a huge range of mountains, then a giant lake, on the left was Thunder's castle! The River Of Poison, everything was there, along with the dark side of Olympia. It was kind of a digital map, when you cross places, the places crossed would vanish! Their location was also marked by a small faded red marker the size of a skittle which camouflaged with the reddish colour of their area. This was a very big advantage for the three. Jay showed it once more to everyone and Partha.

Gita mesmerised at the exquisite detail of the map right down to the tiny trees and canals. 'You know, you are sometimes clever.'

Partha took the map and started studying it carefully. She found out that they were currently quite a distance away from the real entrance of The Land Of Phantoms. They started walking, feeling a bit more confident. But still apart from the map, there wasn't much of a clarity in what they were doing.

Jay turned back and noticed the amount of waste they had crossed. 'Do we even have a plan now?'

'Eh,' scoffed Partha. 'We'll figure that out as we come by. This map will prevent us from getting lost.'

'Seriously? What happened to the "we must have a plan" and stuff?'

'This map was a big find, Jay. I am happy to at least not get lost.'

'Fair enough.'

As he started walking again, Partha stopped him. 'Wait!'

Jay was getting impatient. 'What?'

'We're going in the wrong direction.' Partha pointed towards their north-west side. 'This way to the Land Of The Phantoms.'

~CHAPTER FIVE~

The Little King Returns

Everyone started walking towards their north-western side towards *The Land Of The Phantoms* as Partha had instructed. They were all not aware of the dangers in the land so they had to be cautious at all times. Slowly, the clouds started changing into blood orange, grey and a little tinge of purple. The sand was now a more darkish red, and a few dunes on the way. There were volcanic mountains, a few trees with withered leaves and some with none at all. According to the map, they had to walk quite a bit, till they appeared at the start of The Land Of Phantoms, but the map didn't show what divides both the hemispheres, which remains a mystery.

'Who do you think could be the guardian?' asked Jay.

'I honestly have no idea,' replied Partha. 'It has a high possibility of being a phantom itself. But other than that there is no information.'

'Well, let's just be glad the cousins didn't come,' said Gita.

Jay nodded in agreement.

As the sand was becoming darker with every step, there also appeared a few broken down huts towards their sides. Some roofs were half broken. Some walls had come down as ruins. But still, the size of the huts were pretty big. It looked like it was a comfortable place to live in, once. They passed about ten to twenty huts before they arrived at a river which glowed in its rich green hue. It looked pretty inviting at first, but these three knew the dangers of this river. It was a river completely covered with toxic green poison which will disintegrate anything when touched. Many creatures got caught in that river except for the large butterflies who carefully detected it with their antennae. Sweet innocent creatures like rabkeys too got caught in the river. If they looked beyond it, they could faintly see a cheerful-looking neighbourhood which was quite rare in this atmosphere.

Jay looked at Partha. 'This way?'

Partha nodded, her mind formulating how to cross the river.

Anyone who arrived at this river would have given up instantly to try and cross it but Jay knew a little trick. He walked up to the river and put his sword in it. The glowing green hue got parted into two poisonous lakes on either side of a red and brown pathway.

Partha looked at the pathway and gave a smug smile. 'Neat.'

It was not a long walk and in a short time, they had crossed the river. Jay touched the tip of the sword on the ground of the pathway between the two bodies of water and the river became one again.

Now, the three turned towards the neighbourhood in front of them. They could now see it with clarity. There were a few houses which were of relatively the same size and did not cross the hip height of the trio. They were made of brick and wood like a regular house. There were many ornaments on the outside to decorate the house. The whole area was much nicer than the area surrounding it. It seemed like the creatures who lived here took care of the gloomy atmosphere and one could only imagine how much Thunder would hate this place.

'What is this place?' asked Jay.

'It's the gnome kingdom,' answered Partha, scanning the cheerful scene.

'Oh…the gnomes. We met them four months ago,' said Gita.

Jay took a look at the map Partha was holding and started walking in the right direction. 'Okay then, let us cross this land and get this over with.'

They nodded and started walking, and taking careful accounts of their location.

After a couple of steps, Gita saw some bushes moving. 'What was that?'

'What was what?' asked Jay.

Gita realised that could just be a trick of her mind. 'Nothing.'

They started walking again, slightly more cautious of what's happening around them. Then suddenly, Jay felt a small prickle in his elbow as if something was tossed at his hand. 'Ow!' he cried. He reached out for his elbow and took out something which looked like a needle to him. The needle had a pointy end and two arrow symbols of the other end. The pointy part caused a little pain in Jay's elbow. On the arrow there was a small symbol that said something that Jay couldn't see properly.

'This looks like a tiny arrow.'

Gita frantically looked around. 'That can't be good.'

As if on cue, everyone heard a battle cry which was said with a squeaky voice. Suddenly, thousands of tiny little munchkin-like people marched towards them in suits which looked like they were loaded with protective gear. They were weird little people. They had long ears and noses. They all had hats where the words '*GNOME*

ARMY' were typed in bold, golden letters. The gnomes started attacking the three. Before Gita, Jay and Partha could do anything, a gigantic rope (to the gnomes at least) was tied around each of the three. This rope prevented them from getting the weapons out of their respective scabbards and quivers.

Partha realised it immediately. 'The Rope Of Rangers.' She tried shouting as loud as she could but the gnomes didn't even flinch. They should have been wearing their ear buds. Smart. 'Don't even move,' she told Gita and Jay, who also had some experience with this deadly rope.

The three watched helplessly as the gnomes slowly came and put a similar coloured red cloth on their mouths.

After everything was secure, they started attacking them. All the gnomes gathered together in hundreds of straight lines with their weapons in their tiny little hands. It was like a formal send off. Partha was wondering why the gnomes weren't shooting them yet. They were just standing in their positions, ready to fire.

She tried talking even though she knew it was of no use.

'Mmm...mmm..mm…!'

Jay and Gita didn't understand a word she said. 'Mmm..mm?'

Partha cursed her luck. She couldn't believe that she was attacked and was about to be killed by a bunch of gnomes. Creatures which she could destroy with one swift move of her sword and her foot.

Suddenly, everybody moved aside and left a path. Their commander stepped forward and ran towards Partha, Jay and Gita.

Gita started mumbling furiously. It looked like she was trying to tell them that they meant no harm to the gnomes. But the cloth on her mouth was stuck on tight.

'Sagaster! Shush our guests!' the commander ordered.

One fat gnome came forwards and started scurrying towards the three captures of the gnomes. He had particularly different features from the other gnomes. His hair was chocolate-brown in colour while the common colour of the gnomes was black. His legs and hands were short and his cheeks looked red and chubby. He faltered whenever he moved his legs to walk or run. He looked like he had just drunk a gallon of wine. His eye-balls were not fixed at one position and it moved all about. He finally went up to the commander with great difficulty and saluted. 'Yes sir!'

He went and shot three arrows at a time at each of them. One of them hit Jay's stomach and two more hit his thigh. He belched forward in pain. Even though those arrows were small, they were very painful.

Both Gita and Partha were only hit in the thigh except for one arrow that hit Gita's forehead. Blood started oozing out of a small hole on the skin. How would you feel if a small needle poked a hole in your body? Yep, painful right? That's exactly how Jay and Gita felt.

The commander was satisfied. 'Good. Now you may go back to your position.'

Sagaster went back to his position a little faster this time.

'Ah…what charming guests!' the commander said with a cunning grin. His voice was pretty low but he was much audible both to the gnomes and Gita, Partha and Jay.

Gita was mumbling either in pain or wanting to convince the commander to let her go as she meant no harm.

'What is that?' the commander grinned. 'You want to be assassinated for invading our kingdom?'

Gita didn't stop her mumbling.

'Of course, missy. Don't weep.'

'If you don't know, my name is Jadaister, the commander of the Gnome Army. Also the person who is about to bring out your demise. Our gnome army is equipped with the finest of ballistae. Am I right, my friends?'

'Yeah!' the whole army cheered. It sounded like just ten people were cheering when actually ten thousand gnomes were in a chorus.

After a lot of cheering, the gnomes quieted down.

Jadaister turned back to his captives. 'But unfortunately I can't kill you yet. Rules say that the king shall set eyes on the captive and consent the assassination. So, if the king decides you are too kind to die, he'll free you but that's almost impossible so don't get your hopes up.'

Jay and Gita silently rejoiced. Gignos knew them so they hoped he would set them free.

'I hate that rule!' continued Jadaister. 'Why does the king have to acknowledge everything? Plus half the time, he's late!'

Suddenly, a loud horn (which wasn't that loud for Jay, Partha and Gita) was heard on the grounds. All the gnomes saluted and stood in attention, this time a little more seriously and parted so that a huge path was created. In the path came a beautiful, red chariot in which four thin and elegant gnomes were the charioteers. The chariot was pulled by a baby griffin which matched the colour of the chariot. Even though the griffin was a little one, it was as big as an eighteen-wheeler. Even though the griffin was young, he looked quite ferocious. His eyes were red with anger, probably with all the whips he had got. The griffin halted, and one man got down from the chariot. Behind him, came at least 60 gnomes, and cleared their throats. They unravelled a scroll, and started singing. And the words were:

'He crossed many mountains,
and oceans and caves
But he treated us like friends,
Wealth, and homes and love he gave.
Gracefully decorating the throne,
He made sure no one in his kingdom was left alone!
His stories are many,
He is a warrior,
He gave every penny,
With him the land became merrier.
He is the king,
Prosperity he would always bring,
He punishes the bad,
Donated anything he had,
He was great at everything!
With a king like him,
Not one of us is dim...

The three could hear the song clearly up to this point, as there were almost hundred gnomes which sung it, but now, there was no chance for them, as all the gnomes became quiet except for one gnome. Though it was yelling for his fellow gnomes, the words the three could make out were:

'The greatest of grea-s,
the most powerful gnome!
The slaye-of injusti….
Here he com..s, the twenty eighth king of gno..es..
The Great GIGNOS!'

Gignos came out of his chariot and the army remained still, saluting. 'Where are the prisoners?' Gignos asked. As usual, Chanskein was following him like a personal assistant.

A gnome came forward, showing signs of respect to the king. He pointed at the tied up Jay, Gita and Partha. 'There, your sire.'

'By the way, Jadaister, I am right on time, all the time. And I have to acknowledge everything because I don't want stupids like you killing everyone as per your liking.'

Jadaister looked embarrassed and shuffled nervously. 'No... master, I...didn't mean it….like that.'

Gignos ignored him and turned around. He saw Gita, Jay and Partha tied towards but of course he didn't know that it was them because of the rope and the cloth which was covering their bruised lips.

'They look a lot familiar,' he thought. 'I feel like I've seen them somewhere…'

'Jadaister! Open their cloth covering their mouth!'

The commander was taken aback at Gignos' order. 'But…master. Why?'

Gignos put his ear buds on just in case. 'Don't question me! Just do it!'

Jadaister had no choice but to obey. With sheer anger, he ripped open the cloth.

Everyone sighed, able to breathe better.

'It's me, Jay, who saved you four months ago! We come in peace!'

Gignos recalled the incident four months ago when Stoming put them in a bubble and helped him and his army cross Lake Creaturas. He felt quite angry at his army and commander even though he knew they were just following orders

He turned around, showing his angry face. 'What is the meaning of this?'

The others couldn't connect the dots in their mind, as it was Gignos who ordered to imprison any prisoner who entered.

'Prisoners your majesty! Prisoners who stepped foot in our land!' a soldier shouted.

'They are not prisoners! They are our saviours!' shouted Chanskein.

Gignos gave him a stern look but didn't mind. 'Yes, I agree, Chanskein.'

Gignos turned back to Gita and Jay's attention.

'Sorry, giants...err...friendly giants,' Gignos apologised to them. And he turned to his army once again. 'Guards! Free them! And you better not call them prisoners once more or you'll be sorry!'

The soldiers did as told. They removed the ropes and gags one by one with astounding teamwork. Gita, Jay and Partha did a few hand

and wrist exercises to loosen up which felt much better. They nursed the spots they were shot in and were good to go. The gnomes watched all this silently. Jay knelt down to Gignos, when thirty gnome soldiers surrounded their king, still thinking that the three were harmful, judging by their appearance. A sword and a determined face, tyrannosaurus sized body. What would you feel if a person looked like that? That's how the poor soldiers felt. Gignos ordered his soldiers to make way. He walked all the way near Jay, who let his hand out. Gignos leisurely climbed Jay's hand and stood, balancing himself. He looked at Jay's giant oval eye. He put his hand into his pocket and started foraging something. Finally, he drew out a mini-leaf, almost the size of a thumbprint. The leaf looked golden and was wrinkled. He gave it to Jay, who didn't have a clue what Gignos was giving. Though he received it gratefully and put it into his pocket, deciding not to ask Gignos what it was.

'Looking at your pale face, I guess you don't know what it is,' said Gignos.

'Who doesn't know what a golden leaf is?'

Gignos grinned like a Cheshire cat, which was followed by a chuckle. He looked at Jay and the others with a smile, and a tricky expression which no one could understand.

'You may want to let me down. I'm losing my balance,' Gignos vocalised.

He was back to his normal expression when Jay lowered his hand down to the ground. Gignos vaulted to the ground as the other gnomes shielded him again.

Jay smirked. 'Well, a leaf is a nice gift to give.'

Gignos smiled after Jay and said, 'Consequences will teach you, my friendly giant.'

'Will it, really?'

'You will see,' replied Gignos. 'Anyway, what brings you to my kingdom?'

'Nothing particularly in your kingdom,' replied Partha. 'We just want to cross it, to travel to another land.' She was careful not to mention the Land of the Phantoms as it was a sore subject to the gnomes considering their history.

Gignos smiled. 'Good luck on your journey, he said. 'Don't lose the leaf. You will need it.'

Jay and Gita waved to the gnomes and noticed that the soldier gnomes were still having a grumpy expression. They started walking slowly and noticed that the soldiers were safely escorting their king. Jadaister was still suspicious of the three when they started to move on. Now, the gnome army just looked like a small army of ants to them. They started to move on as fast as possible and there was the sky, turning darker and slowly blending from an orange to a dark purplish-blue. The night was near.

~CHAPTER SIX~

Creepy Toys

They had walked so much that night that they couldn't feel their legs. The last few green mountains in the horizon had vanished, and all they could see before them was red, dry sand, with not a hint of moisture in it, trees without leaves, and large craters here and there. Jay felt like he was on Mars. It was really fascinating, how a single planet could have two large, different biomes. One didn't feel like the other. It was almost as if they were entering an all new planet. Partha was frantically revolving her head, when Jay noticed her.

'What's the matter?' asked Jay.

'It's not like there is a hotel near here. What will we do for the night?'

'We got sleeping bags,' replied Gita, taking out a roll from her bag just to make a point.

'Sleeping bags won't be enough. A fire-breaking eagle can come and turn us into ashes while we are sleeping. No, no, we need a shelter, fast.'

After hearing Partha, Jay decided to start looking out for places of rest as he unfurled the map from his pocket. The same way like the last time, figures and symbols started to appear on the piece of dirty parchment as if it was magic. The peculiar figures and symbols changed colour slowly from a faint brown to a bold black, with a very little part of the prosperous side of Olympia. The lush green hills and the canopy of trees in Glofa forest had vanished, not only in reality, but also in the map. Then, a flag-like label faded in, with some letters appearing on it. It said, 'Homeland of Gnomes' and the flag was continuously waving. He gave a timorous sigh and put the scroll back into his pocket. The sky was turning much darker and the three were getting a bit anxious.

Jay stared at the dark gloomy sky. 'Well.... Sleeping bags may do.'

Partha turned back after hearing Jay's comment. The red could be seen in her eyes. She was for sure aggravated. 'Why don't you understand, you idiot?' WE WILL GET KILLED!' she screamed.

'What a stupid, just like his father.' Partha muttered this quite softly but not soft enough. Both Gita and Jay heard it.

Before Gita could even say a word, Jay pounced at Partha. 'You better not talk about my father like that!'

'Well ...the truth hurts,' said Partha.

Even Gita was quite insulted by Partha's choice of words. 'Okay, first of all, you don't have the right to talk like that. Second of all, don't get angry every few minutes. I can come up with so many insults about your father that you might NOT want to hear.'

Partha was quite taken aback but she didn't stop. 'Your family doesn't deserve to be chosen. You are simply weak.'

'Says a girl who has been imprisoned by Thunder himself.'

This made Partha lose it. She took out her sword and slashed hard at Jay and Gita. In that fraction of a second, Jay took out his own sword and blocked her strike. He didn't want to go to the extent of fighting but he was still mad. He just kept blocking her strikes, but was showing his anger through those blocks. Gita almost took out her bow and arrow, but she decided not to. She understood that Jay didn't want to engage in a duel.

It took some time but Partha finally calmed down. One could see it, as her strikes were losing power gradually until she completely pulled her sword away.

'Is that it?' asked Jay, with a bit of anger in his voice. 'I thought you wouldn't retreat till you stabbed me in the heart.'

'Look…' started Partha when Jay interrupted.

'No. You literally tried to stab me with your sword! It was not going through me.'

'Look, I just lost my mind for a bit. I didn't really mean it. I understand how you feel about your father. I feel the same way. Even I lost my mother. I shouldn't have talked about your father that way.'

'Yes,' chimed Gita. 'You shouldn't have.'

Partha nodded. 'Well we need to find a shelter ... other than sleeping bags...of course.'

They started scouting around for a shelter once again but it was getting darker and darker, they were aware of it. At one point, it would be too dark to see anything.

But luckily and surprisingly, Gita stumbled upon a cave-like structure. I wasn't as visible but she could make out an opening and a relatively big rock on the outside which she hurt her foot on. At first, she was nursing her foot, and when she looked in the front, she totally forgot about her foot. It didn't take long for the others to notice it either. As soon as their gazes were fixed to the opening, they immediately started walking towards it to explore it.

'It's quite dark,' said Gita.

'We have no choice. We will have to find a place before the creatures start hunting,' replied Partha.

They moved a few obstructions at the opening of the cave.

Gita started digging her pocket.

'What are you doing?' whispered Jay.

'I kind of brought a little pocket torch. I have been carrying it since the last time we entered this planet.'

She finally fished it out and switched it on. The light was bright and shone on a stone wall. She moved the torch a little away and saw that there was nothing inside the cave. There was faded red sand on the floor and the cave was about the size of a middle-class bedroom. The stone walls were of a dull grey colour and it was a type of cave you'd expect to find in the dark side. They entered the cave with the help of Gita's torch, watching every single step.

They started to walk deeper inside the cave and found that it was the perfect place to rest, especially for travellers and explorers stuck here. Jay walked to the corner of the cave. He put his hand forward and felt the uneven, stony wall. Gita was still holding the torch, and the light was his only assurance that a petrifying creature wouldn't pop out.

'This is our place,' decided Gita, once again scanning the room with her torch.

'Quite better than I expected,' replied Partha. She sat down with a sigh as Jay and Gita did too. But Gita couldn't help searching the room one more time. She was glad she did. In the corner of her eyes, she spotted a small opening in the wall opposite to them. It wasn't visible at first, but when you saw it, it was very easy to find. There were some dark, soot-covered wooden logs, which blended with the colour of the cave.

'Look,' Gita pointed with her torch. Jay and Partha followed the torch light.

Jay was astonished. 'Is-Is that a fireplace?' It looked exactly like a fireplace which had already been used maybe a lot of months ago, due to the traces of soot and ash around.

'I guess so,' replied Partha. How could there be a used fireplace? All the more in a place no one would wish to go! Anyway, it was an advantage for them. They can't switch on the torch and spend the whole night with it can't they? The three didn't want to analyse it deeper. They had just wanted some warmth as the weather was turning colder.

'Does that mean we can use it?' asked Gita.

'Well, we can,' replied Jay. 'If we figure out how to light it. We can't just rub two pieces of wood together continuously until it lights. I'm already too tired for that.'

But Gita had an idea. She went to the fireplace. She slowly unscrewed the mirror at the end of the torch and placed it on the ground. The torch was pretty strong, even though it was a pocket sized one which is what made her use this idea. She took the torch in one hand and the mirror in the other. She shone the torch onto the mirror and she could see a relatively bright spot of light appearing on the cave walls. She shone a torch at an angle and after a bit of adjusting, the bright spot of light shone on the firewood. Now, she waited. A few sparks lit up but they immediately got put out.

She called Jay. 'Jay! Come here!'

Jay walked up to Gita, after a bit of haggling.

'Now, rub these logs of wood together,' said Gita.

Jay looked at her as if she was crazy. 'That won't work here. The wind is too much.'

'Just trust me.'

Jay plopped down next to Gita. He led the logs by their edges and started rubbing them against each other. After a few seconds, the light, friction and the sparks combined to make a healthy, bright fire. Gita smiled in satisfaction.

Jay was not expecting that at all. As soon as the fire lit, he dropped the logs immediately in shock.

As Partha felt the warmth and light of the fire, she scurried towards the two. 'Where did you learn that?'

Gita turned around to look at Partha. 'Nowhere. Just an idea I guess.'

Partha was impressed. 'That was smart.'

'Yes, yes,' replied Jay. But he was more focused on warming himself. He calmly lay his hands near the fireplace, letting the warm air soak through his skin, enter his veins and transport him into a land of dreams as he dozed off....oh wait, he was in a creepy forest where there was a hundred percent chance of him getting attacked by fierce monsters. No way.

He sighed. All he wanted to do was to spend time with his family and for Thunder and Olympia not even to exist. Those were just ruining his life. Like killing or capturing someone he loved. He just kept his hands near the warm fire. This calmed his nerves. Many thoughts were jogging into his mind along with worries of the future. He didn't even know where his father and his cousins were. Of course he knew that they would return safely. But there were many other worries in his mind which would have to wait. Right now, everyone needed his help. The people of Olympia and his family and friends. He needed to end the rule of Thunder to save them. Though all those thoughts were put aside as they warmed up near the fireplace. Soon, it was time for a long doze off.

Partha felt quite uncomfortable, though. 'Are you sure this is soft enough?'

'Positive,' replied Jay.

'Trust us,' Gita assured. 'We have done this a million times.'

Partha went into the covers and sighed in relief. 'Ahhh…this feels good.'

Jay grinned. 'Told you.'

The sleeping bag had a pillow for the head which was filled with soft cotton. The blankets were quite soft and they came in different colours as well. Jay had a green one, Partha had a blue one and Gita had a magenta colour.

The fire was still burning heartily. It hadn't gotten any fainter. The firewood was setting into an ash black in colour as the fire soared up high into the fireplace. Gita and Jay aligned their sleeping bags with Partha's and went into it. The temperature was getting colder and colder so it was quite warm under the covers.

But Partha suddenly realised something. She peeped out from under the covers and shook Gita and Jay awake.

'What?' asked Gita, groggily.

'Don't we need someone to guard us?' asked Partha.

'We aren't little children, we have the fire.'

'How's the fire going to help us? In fact, it might attract more creatures for a satisfying dinner.'

Gita realised her point. 'Fine… Who's going to guard us?'

'We need to take shifts. Each of us will be awake for some time to keep watch while the others are sleeping in the cave.'

'Ok…'

'And Jay, you get the first shift,' said Partha.

Jay was still half asleep and had barely listened to the conversation. He could only make out "Jay" and "shift".

'Me? Why?' he asked.

'Just do it. It's better to wake up now or else I'm going to have to wake you up again later.'

'Fine…' replied Jay.

He got out of his sleeping bag (much to his dismay) and went towards the opening, still not able to walk properly. He went out through the hole using Gita's flashlight to aid him. A few minutes after he went out, he peeped into the hole to see the faces of Gita and Partha and their whole bodies into the covers.

'Coast is clear,' he said.

After getting that cue, there wasn't much of a visible difference but Jay assumed they heard that and now they're asleep. Jay went out again and began to keep watch. He had his sword with him. He began his wait. He waited and waited till he actually felt like he wanted some monster to attack, just for some action. His hands felt numb from constantly polishing his sword. When his shift just had an hour to go, he slowly closed his eyes for a rest. He slowly dozed off completely. During a really wonderful dream Jay was having, he felt a pat on his shoulder and a voice. 'Jay! Jay!' Slowly it got louder and louder. He woke up with a start. 'AAAHH! Monster!'

'Ugh…I don't know why I didn't expect you to doze off,' the voice replied. When Jay opened his eyes, he saw Partha standing in front of him with folded hands. She had dark circles under her hair and her brown hair was spiked as if she was given an electric shock.

'You don't look like you woke up by yourself,' replied Jay.

'I didn't. You were giving a speech about something. The *'THANK YOU! THANK YOU! I COULDN'T HAVE DONE IT WITHOUT YOU! MY FANS!'* woke me up. Though, your sister is still sleeping. She sure can sleep through a hurricane.'

Jay was quite embarrassed. Gita used to mock him hearing his dreams a *lot* of times.

Partha changed the topic. 'By the way, unfortunately, it's my shift now. You can continue your dream in a bit.'

'Finally. I was so bored. And the sleeping environment is not acceptable.'

Partha smiled and took out her bow and arrow from her quiver, ready to face any monsters. Jay went back into the cave and snuggled into his sleeping bag next to Partha's empty one. He quickly dozed off under the covers.

After a few hours, Partha's shift was done. She tip-toed into the cave and woke up Gita silently. She was careful not to wake up Jay who was muttering something in his sleep which wasn't audible. 'Gita! Gita! Wake up!' she whispered.

Gita didn't move or get up. Partha thought for a moment and got an idea. She went towards Gita's ear and blew some air into it. Gita woke up, startled. She felt slightly ticklish due to the air in her ear.

'Hey! Why did you wake me up? I was having a really spectacular dream!'

Partha sighed. 'Like sister, like brother. Anyway, both Jay's and my shifts are over, so it's your turn now.'

'Already? Ok…' Gita got up from her sleeping bag and yawned. With great difficulty, she went out of the covers. Partha went into her sleeping bag and lay down cosily. She went into a deep sleep in a matter of minutes.

Gita went out of the hole. Partha and Jay were happily in their sleeping bags, pulled into a sound sleep. Whereas, Gita had to get out for her shift. She slowly pushed away the rock which was blocking the entrance with great force. She peeked out, sensing any danger which might lurk near the cave. There was not a creature in sight and Gita was convinced that the coast was clear. She stepped out slowly, still cautious. Amidst the creepy distant howling, rustling of dry leaves and a dripping sound of water made it even eerier. She just sat down on a rock which was shaped oddly with a dent in the middle which provided a reasonably comfortable place to sit on. She sat down as if the rock was a beanbag. With the faint sound of Partha and Jay snoring, she started keeping watch. An hour passed. She was just stationary on the rock with her eyes deeply open. She looked incredibly sleepy as a strange pink hue was around her eyeballs. She looked like she had been bored to death. Another hour passed. Gita was getting very bored but she kept busy by studying the faded red sand that was present in a huge heap near the rock that closed the cave. Her eyes were sinking down as she longed for a peaceful sleep. She just sauntered a few steps back and forth, and hummed another tune just to engage herself from the boredom. At first it was quite eerie for her. But after a couple of hours, the howls and the eeriness sounded like nothing. That was when there was a break of a twig, but this was not scary to her. Later, there was another plop. Well…it must be a stone falling…she had thought. After a few seconds, another sound came. This grabbed her attention. She slowly scampered forward, looking around carefully. She walked more and turned back, just to see if she still had track of the root back to the cave. She thought there was nothing and convinced herself as she just started to walk back near the cave to continue her tunes. She had moved two or more steps, when she stomped on something soft and squishy. Now she was frightened. Would it be some kind of Olympia-creature? Or just some old-normal frayed woollen jacket? She withdrew her leg from the thing and slowly looked down. To her relief, it was just a soft little teddy bear! But the condition it was in was awful. More than awful, it was pitiful. It had torn in a lot of places, with its cotton-stuffing oozing out. Its ear was almost dangling, with a huge stitch across its face. It also wore a ragged shirt. But she couldn't identify its colour in the dark, but it looked like some kind of old dark-green. It also had a small, dirty bow-tie in its chest and all the buttons were broken, while some were not even there. The white colour of it had totally turned grey, after many brown spots of some kind of stain all over the back. It was creepy-looking but looked like it was a very cute plush toy. Gita was taken aback. This reminded her of her old teddy bear which Bingo said was the last present from her mother. But now it was not a time for these sentiments. She had to find out what the thing was. So, she slowly lifted it and took it near her face. She decided to take the poor toy back to the cave to show it to Jay and Partha, who would be really fascinated. But, something was odd. A toy? In this state? In the middle of the entry of the darkest side on the planet? It wasn't good. After all, she didn't want to get them into trouble, and thought that it might be dangerous.

Keeping the toy down, she said, 'Rest here…I am sorry.'

She took her attention off the toy and walked back for guarding. After all, it was a toy she thought. But then there was another stunner. There were many other toys in the same old state randomly appearing in places! Not only teddy-bears, but all kinds of dolls and toys. There was an old car doll, with one of its wheels missing, a tennis racket, with all its strings jumbled up, and many, many more countless others. There was something odd in all these happenings. She decided not to waste her time inspecting each and every toy, and ran back without looking down. But the toys started multiplying faster than expected. Gita had to use her athletics skills to dodge all the toys in her way. But more and more toys appeared and it became harder and harder to dodge. Then a strange thing happened. The teddy bear which she had lifted up came alive! It stood up on two legs with two sharp fangs shooting out of its mouth. It started to run near her and hopped to her leg.

'AHHH!' screeched Gita. 'JAY! PARTHA!'

Jay and Partha barely opened their eyes. They just heard a faint voice which they assumed was a trick of their minds. For them, the only thing which he knew was that Gita was just standing out half-asleep and guarding at times. Now it was too late. Every single toy which had piled up came alive, with each of them having some sort of a terrifying element. Some had fangs, some started developing spikes and overall, it looked absolutely spine-chilling. The teddy bears and other figures hopped on Gita, just leaving her a tiny hole to breathe. The cars and other vehicle toys were running around wildly. The teddy bears were looking like their leader. But "teddy bears" were too nice a name to give them.

Gita shouted louder this time. 'JAY! PARTHA!'

Now they had to hear it. Partha was still drowsy and had barely gotten up but Jay woke up even before Partha could process what was going on. He got up and pushed away the rock like he was opening a curtain and Partha was not far behind. They scanned the surroundings and saw the pile of toys and Gita's legs sticking out. Horrified, they sprinted towards Gita and pushed away the toys with their swords. But it was of no use. The toys which should have been dead by now just got back up and scurried towards the three, without missing a beat. The toys started to hop on Jay and Partha too, like they had done on Gita. The sword had fallen to his right and had no way of getting it back. He used all his power to reach it, but when he almost touched the handle, a crocodile toy bit one of his fingers. He withdrew his hand immediately, and noticed that he was bleeding. Now they were surrounded by toys, like ants feeding on its prey. He knelt down and knew that they were only dependent on Partha.

'PARTHA!' they both shouted.

This time Partha woke up with a jerk. She ran out swiftly, noticing that the rock was already moved. When she was out, she saw the predicament Jay and Gita were in. At first, she thought of pushing the toys away with her sword. But that would be of no use. These toys would jump on her and she would stand crying out for help for others. Amidst all the trouble, she took a stone and hit down which caused some noise. The toys turned still. Their faces were pale and turned back to glare at Partha's face. Now, all the toys had got off of Jay and Gita, joining the other pale ones. They stood still and Jay and Gita were frozen too. Suddenly, all the toys combined to form a massive army of toys and started to run towards Partha with full angry faces.

'Oh no,' commented Jay. He took his sword and pushed off a few as Gita used her hands, as she couldn't aim the toys in motion with her arrows. Suddenly, Gita thought of something. She twitched her eyebrows and looked at Jay's face. Her eyes were bright and confident, as she raced down to Partha and stood in front of her as a barrier. Jay was surprised by Gita's action, but didn't know what she was about to do. The other toys halted immediately, panting, with furious faces. Everyone in the scene was clueless of what was happening except Gita. She knelt down on her knees and clearly saw the teddy bear which she had put down. The angry face of it slowly started to poise. She took her hands towards the teddy bear and lifted it gently by its waist. Fortunately, every single teddy had started to cool down, thinking that Gita meant no harm, which was true. She took the teddy bear near her face and gave a joyful smile.

'Gita,' called Jay. 'What are you doing?'

Partha immediately shushed Jay with a finger over her mouth. Then, she backed off and signalled Jay to do so as well. She didn't know why, but she trusted Gita. Just an instinct, I guess.

Gita brought the toy to her face and gave a warm kiss on its forehead and that was when a miracle happened. The toy's face suddenly turned sad. It was living its rough past, when it got thrown away by its owner and ended up here. It literally had tears about to roll in its marble eyes. Its long fangs slowly started to shorten. All its stitches blended together. Its dangling ear fixed itself as Gita left it down. Now it looked really *beautiful.*

Gita still didn't take her smile off her face and stood up on her feet. Now, the beautiful teddy bear joined hands with the other one. The other turned beautiful too! Then the other one…the chain continued. Now, all the ugly, loathsome, toys had turned beautiful and new!

'Clearly, love heals everything doesn't it?' said Gita with a smile. Even a smile grew in Partha and Jay's face. They ran towards Gita and hugged her. They both looked down and even smiled at the toys. Now all the toys had a satisfied smile on their faces. Slowly, all the toys which had smiled started to vanish to golden dust! Everything started to vanish as the last one which Gita had met had also reached the heavens.

~CHAPTER SEVEN~

The Vulture Of Flames

As the long march towards dawn continued, the sun was a lot more out in the northern horizon, but that wasn't the greatest worry. If they had managed to survive till the sun was out, it was of no use, as the dark clouds were piling up in the northeast which is where they were headed. The last night was quite miserable, and they were sure that everything could have gone good if the start had been as sweet as the end. Partha and Jay had gone to sleep after the entire incident whilst Gita continued her shift. After her shift was over, she immediately entered the warm cave and woke up Jay and Partha. They quickly freshened up and began to get ready to continue their quest. They lifted their sleeping bags and packed them into the bag. The three decided to carry the bag along with them, as they still didn't know how many days they were going to rummage through the land without anything suitable for life. Even though they knew that they couldn't get any sleep when they were in the heart of the dark side, they carried it around just in case. Jay took the map and Partha took the bag as they trotted out of the cave. Gita closed the cave with the rock as a new day had officially begun.

Almost half an hour had passed. Jay and Gita had been following Partha, who was at least twenty metres ahead. Obviously, they knew that she would be feeling as tired as they were, but she didn't show it in her face. She was just taking a long walk, the same as a morning walk. Jay was just staring at the map, which had a compass which spanned on its own. But to everyone's dismay, the part beyond the dark grey clouds wasn't displayed yet.

'Well what were those things?' Jay asked.

'Toys,' replied Partha. She wasn't really interested in the topic. So Jay turned to Gita.

Gita saw Jay's questionable expression. 'Well, it was pretty obvious.'

'How?'

'When kids throw away their toys, they appear here in the Dark Side. They are nice to people who are nice to them. They just appear here out of nowhere. Nowadays, since there are no more kids at Olympia, these toys are endangered. We just saw one of the few packs.'

Partha barely heard the conversation. 'I think we need to get a move on guys.' The quest continues…

***

Luckily, Bingo had stopped sneezing after quite a long time. They were still quite far away from the castle of Thunder. The cousins were feeling quite calm and cheerful while Bingo was expectedly worried sick about Jay, Gita and even Partha. Az was also pretty calm and was mindlessly chatting with the cousins. It astounded Bingo how these guys could be so calm. He was continuously muttering:

'I hope they are safe. I hope they are safe,' so much that Az was getting irritated. 'Relax! Our children are just going to a scary dark place with no directions or maps! Nothing to worry about!'

Bingo gave him a scowl. 'Don't you ever worry about children?'

'Believe me, mine has been in a much worse situation than your children.'

Bingo remembered the whole capturing of Partha which had been for a few weeks. He didn't think he would have survived in such a situation. 'Did you feel the same way?' he asked, but this time, more faintly.

'No,' Az said. 'I felt much worse. But at the same time I believed in her. I knew she would return.'

Bingo had decided to keep the topic aside, as it didn't make both of them very comfortable. Their pasts were filled with terrors which others couldn't even dream about. Both their wives had gone missing and they were kept away from their children. But all they had to do was help defeat the ruthless idiot responsible for all this. Thunder.

***

'Our father would have created such a fuss about us,' said Jay, as he tried to make something out of the map. But as usual, the map had turned faulty. No places were clearly visible. The compass was spinning with rage as if there was a magnet next to it. The water would be over in a few hours, but it seemed as if their stomachs were full and weren't hungry, which was really good news. Well, they were wondering what their aimless walk was going to give, but they had decided to follow the dark clouds floating in the distance. The ground started to get more ash-like. There were some red sandy areas here and there like the land of Mars but it wasn't at all as mesmerising. The entire place started reeking with the smell of pure evil and ash. Jay, Partha and Gita were still trying to neglect the putrid smell.

'I hope my dad isn't like that,' said Partha, trying to reduce her frequency of breathing.

'You know, they are just worrying about you, right?' replied Gita. 'It's normal.'

'Yeah. But I just wish he knows that we're safe and sound.'

'Well, I agree with that.'

They were just trying to deviate themselves from the fact that they were in the most dangerous place ever. It was quite hard to differentiate between day and night. The sky looked quite dark during late dusk. The sky was heavy purple with a minuscule tinge of orange. Dark clouds made it difficult to see the purple sky and they just got thicker and thicker as they went on. It looked like it was about to rain but that was just endless darkness. Their clothes were the same they had worn when they teleported here from Earth. They were not much in the mood of changing. The air suddenly started getting hot with the smell of acid ringing in the already toxic atmospheric condition. The three wanted to hurl.

Partha covered her nose. 'Uhh ... What is that acidic smell?'

'I don't know. But it smells so horrible. I suggest covering our nose. I don't think this smell is good for us.'

But the reason was clearly visible. Holes the size of fully-inflated basketballs filled the ground. After looking down and staring at each other's faces covering their noses, they were surprised to see that almost a mile ahead had holes of those kinds. They started to think about how they were going to cross the upcoming distance. All the more, they could barely see the horizon as green smoke was oozing out the lava.

'What are those?' asked Jay in a nasal voice. Even Partha hadn't the faintest.

Gita gulped some saliva as fear ran down her spine. *How were they going to cross all these holes!* She was thinking. No one spoke, as Jay kept a step in between the space between two holes and noticed two bubbles in the boiling lava.

'Ugh,' he commented. Next was Partha. She took a step forward in Jay's footsteps. Jay leaped, crossing a small puddle. Partha tried examining the puddle. Suddenly it just spewed out some fire right on her leg.

'Ouch!' she screeched, and noticed that the part in which the drop had splashed had burnt and she could see her top layer of the skin gone.

'That was really dangerous,' said Gita.

'And seemed painful,' added Jay.

It took some time but they hopped and crossed by all the puddles of lava. But as they were almost done, they noticed a huge puddle, almost the size of a small jeep stagnant in front of them. Jay, as usual, tried to proceed further and was taken aback after seeing bubbles oozing out. They couldn't go around it as many of the same sized ponds were towards their sides as well. Now they were stuck. They wouldn't have even been able to cross the puddle by going around it, as the puddles were slowly starting to get larger every step. Partha pointed straight towards the puddle, after swivelling her head frantically.

Jay saw Partha pointing to the huge puddle. 'You can't expect us to drop into that.'

'There's a rock!' she replied. Jay and Gita peered into the puddle and noticed a rock which was slowly going into the puddle. They had to act fast. And the size of the rock was not too big as well and could barely support one person. Suddenly they found themselves in a real life 'Floor is Lava' challenge.

'There must be another way!' said Jay, not liking the odds. But if they managed to jump onto that, a step would help them make it to the ground.

'Looks like this is the only way,' replied Gita. They looked at their faces for one last time and Partha stood front. She could see her faint reflection on the hot lava, and thought once more if it was truly necessary to take such a risk. She took another step and was ready to jump. With one leap, she made it to the rock safely. And immediately, she jumped into the safe zone. Gita and Jay were relieved as they found it was possible to cross this. Gita stepped front and had a little bit of advantage as she was quite tall, and jumped to the rock, as Partha gave a hand to Gita as she stepped on the ground. Now Jay was the last one to go. *What if I slip and fall into the lava?* He was thinking. With all his strength transmitted to his legs, he hopped onto the rock and lost his footing for a split second. His heart skipped a beat as he immediately regained his footing.

'Be careful!' cried Gita.

'I'm trying!' replied Jay.

The rock was very slippery now and with a leap of faith, he landed on the ground with the help of Partha and Gita. He slowly opened his eyes and looked at Partha and Gita who were holding his hands. He loosened the grip and let out a sigh of relief. They caught some air and started walking. As they went on the smell had slowly started to fade away, and they could breathe some air. They didn't know what was wrong, but the ground was still hot, even after there was not even a single drop of lava in their radius. But they ignored it and marched towards the clouds. There didn't seem to be any danger nearby as the atmosphere was really quiet. Gita turned back, and noticed Jay lagging behind. She waited as Jay absent-mindedly walked to her.

'What's the matter?' she asked, once Jay caught up.

'Nothing.'.

Gita nudged her brother's shoulder. 'C'mon! I am not going to do anything.'

'Fine.' He was about to tell, but something caught his eye. 'Whoa! What is that?' And he started running towards their side.

Partha and Gita immediately started following him. Jay came to a halt at a large rock the size of a curtain. It was mainly grey with a few red and soot stains. The bottom part was quite ashy as well. But it was not the rock he was talking about. It was the thing on the rock. He walked slightly back and stood on his toes so he could see what was on the rock. There the three saw a nest occupying the whole space and inside the nest were two weirdly shaped rocks radiating a decent amount of heat energy. They had a few cracks on them as well, almost as if they were hit by something. They emitted an orange hue which was a bit strange.

'What's that?' asked Gita, as she started climbing the rock.

Partha peered closely but she couldn't make out what that was. But still, there were no 'nice' things in this part of Olympia. 'I don't know. But please get down. I don't think that's safe.'

Gita sighed and got down, believing Partha mostly because she knew Olympia better than her.

But Jay needed to go up. He needed to prove himself. His ego prevented him from listening to Partha. He slowly climbed the rock, catching the scarce foot holes in it. He completely ignored all sounds around him. Once he climbed up, he balanced himself and took a step towards the…thing. He bent down, and lifted up the strange object with both his arms.

'Are you a lunatic?' yelled Partha. 'Come down!'

'Lunatic is it? I am not a person who fears an egg!'

Suddenly, he heard a faint *crack!* He neglected that and put his ear closer and heard something very peculiar like a chirp. He suddenly understood what it was and tried putting the thing down and slowly tried walking away. But it was too late. The object cracked and out of it came an orange chick. It was really adorable and it radiated a decent amount of heat.

Jay realised immediately that the mom might be near and started climbing down as fast as possible. He never shouldn't have gotten up, he thought. He only looked more stupid after this.

Suddenly he heard a cry from Partha, 'Run, you idiot!'

Jay didn't even need to think twice. That was anyway what he was doing. He barely looked up as he jumped from the rock and landed on the ground with a thud. He lost his balance for a few seconds but immediately started sprinting. But by now, he was forced to look up.

Now the three were being chased down by a giant eagle…at least it looked like one… It had flames coming out its body, which looked like its feathers were full of blood red and orange. It was as big as a school bus, and its talons were as sharp as razors. It soared down, trying to catch them like mice. They ran as fast as they could and jumped behind a tree which lacked leaves. Jay ducked down as he recollected the wrong he had done. He had got his own sister, and his friend into great trouble. He couldn't have done anything worse than that. The eagle started searching for them behind every tree as Partha looked at Jay with fury and signalled that he was dead. She was pretty scary when she was angry. Meanwhile, the eagle turned confident that the three had escaped as it flew back to its nest after noticing that her baby had hatched just now.

The three figured it was good to talk.

Even before Gita could take a breath, Partha lost it. 'Jay! Do you have any brains? Huh? You could've killed us! It's called the Vulture of Flames for a reason!'

Gita looked at him with a decent amount of anger. 'That was really foolish, Jay.'

Jay didn't have anything to say.

Partha flicked Jay's head. 'We need a reply, Jay!'

'I ... I am sorry,' replied the faint voice of Jay.

'Well, *now,* we have got to find a way to cross that creature,' said Gita.

Partha was still in a mood. 'Cross it? You are kidding, right? It's going to pick you up like a worm and toss you a mile away!'

'Partha! Calm down! You are not helping,' snapped Gita. 'We need a distraction. What about Jay…' Gita looked to her side to find Jay, but he was gone! Gita looked around the tree and saw Jay running towards the creature. Partha sighed and pulled her sword out and Gita loaded her arrow and ran behind him. Jay jumped towards the creature and slashed at it with his sword. The vulture barely made a sound but glared at Jay. Gita decided to use this. She loaded her arrow and shot it straight to the creature's neck, but unfortunately the arrow disintegrated and fell as ashy dust in front of the vulture. Now Gita was in trouble too. The vulture didn't even notice the arrow and went as Jay. Meanwhile, Jay was quick to act, he rolled over, grabbed his sword and slashed at its neck. At the same time, Partha had come into the scene and Partha slashed her sword at the vulture's flamy body. The creature screeched as a slit opened in the places that the trio slashed in. They realised that this was their chance and started scurrying away. But it was not done yet. The vulture was healing itself! The flames merged together and it looked like there was no harm done. Partha tried to divert the monster to her side, but it was of no use. It flew a few metres towards her, till Jay shouted at the bird which provoked it more.

'Why would you do that!' yelled Partha. 'We can't keep diverting it!' She ran towards Jay and helped him fight it. Gita aimed and shot more arrows, but obviously, nothing happened with the arrows turning into mere dust. She stopped shooting them, as if shot more her quiver would be empty. Jay slashed his sword into the skin as the heat from the bird climbed up the blade and then to his hand.

He yelled in pain. But they had no choice. Gita tried to play her part by throwing stones at the bird but that didn't seem to cause any harm at all. Partha fought it with the sword from her side with all she might do to Jay. But they *had* to think of something which harmed the monster. Something which could *destroy* it totally. Now, the bird went on the offence. I glided up from the ground and soared straight down to Jay. It pushed him with its talons as he fell down and gathered all its force to cut open his chest. Jay was using all his available force and holding the monster's scaly feet, being careful not to touch the flames.

'Jay!' yelled Gita. She knew she couldn't use her arrows. But Partha already charged at the bird. Just as she was about to give a body blow, the bird shrieked with immense pain. Its toes let loose. Jay quickly moved out of the way as the bird fell down, creating a mild tremor. Gita ran up to him and scanned his bruised body. Thankfully, there was no injury. She looked up at the bird. On the bird's neck, there was an arrow. But unlike Gita's normal arrows, this one had a gleam around it. The minute the arrow had touched the surface of the bird, it fainted. All its flames on its body started to freeze. Jay picked his sword up and turned back, still lying down. Gita and Partha also had their eyes fixed behind Jay. There stood a handsome, well-built man, with a little beard and moustache, wearing a black torn shirt, with a tattered, stained coat, with a tight black belt and fit pants which were of the same colour. His brown hair was let loose, and his boots were frayed, and a nice large golden bow, with a collection of arrows filling the quiver. A woman, who was surely feeling cold with ragged clothes, was also hiding behind the man. Jay slowly got up, confident that the eagle wouldn't wake up soon, and slowly limped towards them. He was feeling really dizzy, as whatever he saw appeared double. Gita put her arm around Jay and went with him. Partha too came next to Jay and started helping him get over his dizziness.

'What happened to him?' asked the man.

'What do you think happened?' asked Partha. She pointed at the fallen vulture.

'Oh…,' replied the man. 'That must have hurt.'

The woman came out of hiding and came in front of the well-built man. The three could see her even more clearly now. Jay suddenly stood up straight and looked at Gita. Gita also had a similar reaction. Both of them bolted towards the weak-looking woman and gave her a bear-hug.

'Wh-who are you kids?' the woman asked in a hushed voice.

Gita felt some tears in her eyes. 'Mom! You are alive!'

~CHAPTER EIGHT~

The Golden Sacrifice

'My ... my children?' The woman still looked baffled.

Jay took out a photo in a slightly cracked glass case in Gita's bag and showed it to the woman. The woman stepped back. She was in a daze. Two random children were claiming her as her mother but her apprehension all changed when she looked at her photo. It was her. There was no question about it. She shed a few tears. She thought she lost them fourteen years ago. She thought they were never to be seen again. And here they were. She started sobbing as she took Jay and Gita and trapped them in a warm embrace, now feeling more comfortable. The woman looked at their faces once more and started smiling, as the hug continued. The two didn't know what had happened, how their mother survived, but they knew one thing, their loving mother was alive and that's all they cared about. Jay and Gita withdrew their hands as millions of questions were running through their minds.

How did Thunder let them go? How did she *escape*? Who *was* that man standing beside their mother?

Jay took notice of that man who was washing off some dirt from his quiver. Jay went up to him. 'Who are you? How are you with my mother?'

Gita saw as she went up to Jay, along with Partha and their mother (Asha). The man turned his face and looked up at Jay, Gita and Partha.

Asha started to speak with a weak voice. 'He was part of something called-'

The man interrupted her. 'Not here. We need to be careful of these creatures. They could do some serious damage if we mess with them or their young ones.'

Partha looked at Jay, like a reminder of the scene that took place before these two came.

'I know a safe place. Follow me,' the man said.

'But at least tell-' Jay started but the man showed a sign which meant *'later'*.

Everyone agreed with the man and started walking. Jay and Gita were holding hands with their mother and started talking like one happy family. Partha walked with the man. Partha tried asking the man for some information like *'What was going on?'*, *'Who are you?'*, *'Where are we going?'*, and *'Do you have any food?'*. The man just shrugged her questions off with a mere *'I told you. Later.'* An awkward silence followed that conservation. Where they were going was quite safe ... at least they hoped so. Their feet weren't very tired as they had walked longer distances than this. After a ten-minute walk, a dark grey cave appeared in front of their eyes. It looked quite dirty from the outside and there was red sand everywhere around it. The sand gave the cave a less dull look as it engulfed the cave's borders. The cave appeared to become bigger and bigger as they went near it.

Finally when they reached the cave, the man showed a faint smile. 'We're here.'

The others stared at him like he lost it.

The man had a smile on his face. He looked at the other's blank faces and decided to explain better. 'The cave ... that's what I'm talking about.'

Nobody responded.

The man tried to explain better. 'The cave-'

'We know that this is a cave. What's so *special* about it?' interrupted Partha.

'This is where I and your mother were living for the last 14 years.'

'You *lived* here?' asked Jay. 'We barely survived in a cave for a night!' He looked at his mother who nodded in agreement.

The man was pushed a small rock away from the opening as he revealed the inside. 'Tada!'

The cave-house wasn't very mesmerising but it was cosy enough to live in. I guess that's more than enough when living on the dark side. It had a dusty dining table and three chairs displayed neatly around it. One of the chairs looked like it was horribly bitten by termites. Luckily there were two others which made it the correct amount for Asha and the man.

There were scattered photos of the man, his parents and a woman who looked like his wife. They couldn't make out the baby as it was covered in a blanket and appeared to be sleeping soundly with a stuffed animal at its side. There were more pictures which portrayed a sword which Jay immediately recognised as the sword of Frencher. At the corner, there were three beds and each had a pillow each.

This place looked like it was designed for three. Near the bed, there was a stand in which the man kept his quiver of arrows and his bow. Just next to the dining table was a brown couch which looked like the most comfortable furniture in the room. Even the beds didn't look as comfortable. There was another opening which led to the kitchen. They went into the kitchen to explore it. The kitchen had a stand where a couple of ingredients like tea powder was there. There was a lighter placed on the stand which was mostly used to light up the stove which was on a separate stand. There was a table in the centre where the mixing took place. They all went back to the previous room.

The man plopped down on the couch. 'So ... what do ya think?'

Partha looked around. 'It's a cosy place to live in, actually. Better than I expected.'

The man smiled. 'See! I told ya. Ok ... sit down next to me and I'll tell you everything.'

Everyone plopped down on the couch.

Asha just went into the kitchen to make some tea while the man started narrating his story. 'I am Brej.'

Partha interrupted. 'Hey, I've heard your name! Perhaps, my father often...speaks about some guy called Lashman.'

Brej gasped. 'Who's your father?'

'Azzer.'

'Oh, you are Partha! Az has talked about you when you were an infant!'

'Ahem ... I hate to break the moment here but the story please?' Gita said to Brej.

'Oh. Right. So ... yeah, I am Brej. I am from the board...well I am also a warri-' Brej was about to finish when Partha interrupted.

'Can you please start the story?'

'Very well,' replied Brej.

'It was a long night, a stormy one. We heard a cry entering the castle and a woman weeping. It was A.B.A Stoming, the wickedest man I have ever known-'

'Hey, Stoming's not wicked! He fights against Thunder!'

'Really? Him? I knew that there was a good soul inside him! He and his brother…Hmm…. Ellio! How's he?'

'Still bad,' replied Gita.

'So, dears, you might not want to interrupt again,' spoke Asha, peeping from the kitchen.

'Ok mum.'

'Well…where did I stop? Hmm…No one was allowed in the room of Thunder except Stoming. He was dragging a woman and a man, who were carrying two toddlers. The woman pleaded for forgiveness and the poor souls didn't know a clue why they had been dragged to a different planet. Stoming had just escaped from Alcatraz Prison, as Thunder ordered three men including me and Lashman, my friend, to come in. We went in, obeying the orders of our king, as he ordered us to throw the whole family into the dungeons. Thunder refused to tell the reason, but we had no choice except to follow his wicked rules. We sent the family to the dungeons, as two long months passed. The woman was really pleading to let them out, and every night we used to hear the cry of the toddlers. Lashman and I really wanted to let them escape, but we knew that Thunder would execute us in the most horrible and diabolical way possible. That was the day when Olympia's second war started. Thunder was not really focusing on the family. But even in the war, he didn't fight much. He made us board members and our family fight. I… (Sighs)…lost my family in that war.

Everyone wondered how many people lost their lives in the numerous wars and disasters of Olympia. They felt pretty bad for Brej.

'Anyway ... after the war, Thunder started focusing on the family more. Still, we had no clue of why the family was trapped. The next month, Thunder called Stoming again. They had quite a long chat, as Stoming snatched the toddlers from the family. That was the last day we saw Stoming ... Well, at least for a long time, he didn't show his face in Thunder's castle. He had vanished, but sometimes spoke into Thunder's mind. The woman, who was also your mother, was really depressed and passed out. Thunder didn't care a bit about her medical conditions, but Lashman and I gave her sufficient food and water. We used to comfort her by lying that their children were surely alright. Though, we thought the toddlers were doomed especially on Stoming's watch. But, they had a ray of confidence hidden in them. A few long years passed. I felt as miserable as them as I didn't have a clue where my family was, how they were, even if they were *alive.* Your father and mother were furious as well. They really wanted to know how their children were, but Thunder didn't pay a second to listen to those nonsensical questions ... Well, at least that's what he said. A month had flown by quite swiftly. We knew that the next day would also be as sorrowful as the days were, but something surprising had happened. It was Stoming. He entered, this time not with the toddlers. As usual, Thunder and Stoming had a chat that night. Lashman and I really wanted to know the reason why all these things were happening. We knew that we surely had the right to know. We stuck our ears into the wall, and saw a long creepy shadow on the ground. The weather was really stormy. The lighting and thunder always depicted that something bad was about to happen. We started to listen word by word. He started asking many questions about *Enchanted Books*, and also mentioned that the *Enchanted Book of Wishes* was going to only be pursued by Thunder. He also mentioned that the toddlers were surely the ones destined to get the *Enchanted Books*. Many truths started to unfold. We came to know that the toddlers were surely safe and sound. We ran to the dungeons, to convey the news to your mother and father. They were really happy, and we surely wanted to save the *parents* of the chosen ones as they surely were going to be a great pillar in defeating the vile reign of Thunder. We came up with a plan, making sure that no one was around. The next morning, at the court, Lashman and I, as every day, went to report to Thunder. He was really moody that day, and sure we could guess that he was thinking about a suitable plan to hurt your parents. He was in deep thought when Lashman interrupted. Thunder was really shocked to hear these words from Lashman. Lashman asked if they could kill your parents. Thunder stood up, with a gleeful and appalled expression on his face and let out a wicked grin. He agreed to Lashman and we were happy that everything was going according to plan. I headed back to the dungeons and put up a false-angry-face as Lashman was set to look happy. We dragged your parents to the court. Gritchler had also come with us. We asked Thunder the suitable place to kill the family. He was thinking quite a bit, as Lashman popped out with an idea. He suggested Thunder to throw them in the middle of the dark side, and also said that it was the worst punishment. Thunder gladly agreed and ordered us to throw them as soon as possible, but stopped us when we almost started to go. We were really anxious for Thunder not to doubt us, as we were not going to kill the family, but escape along with your parents. He ordered us again to take Gritchler along with us to kill the two. We almost felt as if the whole plan had been destroyed. He then told us to leave Bingo with him, for a source of information, which felt even worse. Your dad joined the guards back to the dungeons, as we proceeded with Gritchler and your mother. Lashman and I were thinking about an idea to get rid of Gritchler, but we were more engaged in thinking on how to save your mother. We had almost reached the start of the forest. We had to think about something quick. To everyone's shock Lashman did something. An *action* that makes me tell this story to you. He grabbed the arm of Gritchler and yelled at us to run, and he had no choice except to do that. Gritchler made a wound in his leg with his dagger and the Scepls surrounded him. That was the day I felt the cheapest. Seeing a best friend almost die in front of you gave the worst feeling. A feeling you couldn't even dream of. I really wanted to help, but if I did, his sacrifice would be of no use. I knew that Thunder would surely kill him, but I had no choice except to save your mother. I ran with your mother, all across the forest and reached here. We surely have a rough time finding a suitable place to live. After a few months of pain and sorrow, the beheading of Lashman reached my ears. That day my rage started. The rage to kill Thunder...and here we are, fighting for life. Here we are, living the pain of our best friend's death.'

There was a great silence throughout the cave. Asha had sat down after giving everyone tea. So the smell of tea completed the atmosphere. Everyone was moved by the story. Such people were the main reason they were fighting against Thunder. Brej sniffled and got off the sofa. He went to the kitchen to get some water. The others just stood still.

'My dad had told Lashman died for betraying Thunder,' said Partha. 'But I had no idea about all this.'

Brej came out of the kitchen, sipping on the water. 'At the time, Az was working for Thunder as well as a guard. But he was barely included in all this.'

Gita decided to shift to a more comfortable topic. 'What do you do for food?'

'It was really difficult at first. I had to sneak into Olympia and grab fruits and berries from the forest. Sometimes, I even kill some animals.'

Jay grinned. 'Well, mom. You have made history. The only earthling to eat Olympian meat.'

'First of all…why are you guys here?' asked Brej. 'I have never seen kids fighting the Vulture Of Flames!'

'Ahh...That's quite a long story,' said Jay. 'We have already visited Olympia twice, and the first time was when Stoming betrayed us-'

'Betrayed! I thought you just said the guy was good!'

'It is quite a long story. Stoming, from the day he separated us from mother and dad as toddlers, was acting as a false dad. He had kind of transformed into a man who just looked like…our real dad. So, much later, we found a piece of parchment in a lake while fishing.'

'You know fishing?' asked Brej. 'That's all ya need to survive here.'

'I know it…' replied Jay. 'But trust me, I am not fishing ever again.'

'Traumatised,' said Brej. 'I get it.'

Gita continued on for Jay. 'So, that parchment had a clue on it which I don't remember. So at our risk, we went hiking on a mountain and found a teleporter-burrow. That was when Stoming…uh… the false dad grabbed the book to the other side of the burrow, which was also the entrance of Olympia. Then, he transformed into Stoming, and called Thunder. They said that the book grabbed by Stoming was the *Enchanted Book of Wishes.* Then, they tried to kill us but thankfully, our real dad came in a griffin and saved us.'

'And you lost the Enchanted Book of Wishes!'

'We got it back,' said Jay.

'Wait ... how?'

'One day, Stoming came into our house, terribly wounded. He said that Thunder had betrayed him and almost killed him but he managed to escape. We didn't believe him at first but he showed us eye-footage, as we called it. And then we travelled to Olympia to tear the first book and take away his scepter. On the way, we met Az, flew butterflies, fought dragons and then, went to Thunder's castle-'

'You survived in Thunder's castle?' asked Brej. 'He could have killed you! Does he still have Gritchler as his board member?'

'Yep.'

'That rascal!'

'Anyway, Thunder did trap us. But we managed to escape along with everyone in decent shape. We even rescued Partha who was trapped.'

Gita looked at Partha, expecting her to answer. But before she could, Brej interrupted. 'You were captured by Thunder? My god!'

Partha nodded and shuddered. 'Yes. And I don't want to talk about that.'

'Anyway, now Stoming is imprisoned by Thunder and Az, our dad - Bingo and our cousins have gone to save him while we are on a quest to find the Enchanted Book Of Resurrection.'

'Oh…well, be careful of Thunder. That's all I can say to ya. The man is crazy evil,' replied Brej. 'Want some *water berries*?' He walked outside the cave, with everyone following him. To the left of the opening, lay a few large bushes filled with numerous berries. They looked like mini watermelons.

'Water berries?' asked Jay.

'Yep! They are quite scrumptious.' Brej picked up a few and showed it to everyone, expecting them to take a few.

Gita, being quite curious, picked up a berry from Brej's hand and nibbled on it like a rabbit. 'It really tastes like watermelon candy!'

Hearing this, everyone felt safe and picked one for themselves. Asha had come outside and picked a berry from Brej's hand and let the flavour ooze into her mouth. There was happiness all around, giving an elated aura. Finally, after many years, there was happiness around. It wasn't really a good first dinner with a family, but after all the sacrifices, efforts, pains and struggles, they had accomplished one of the many goals they thought was impossible. Seeing their beloved mother again.

~CHAPTER NINE~

Over The Log

Jay and Gita were as ecstatic as ever. It was such a pleasant surprise when they came to know that their mother was still alive and near them. Jay and Gita had sunk to the thigh of their mother for some time. They were just laying down on Asha's lap and catching up with her. Partha was up for some time, gazing at the lifeless sky. She could see her father, mother, and her as a little kid standing in the middle of her parents. The picture of her dad and her mother brought tears to her eyes, as she forgot everything else. The quest, Jay, Gita, the upcoming dangers and so on. She wondered where her mother was, and what had happened to Stoming who had gone to save her. Her imaginative picture of her family faded behind the stars as she could feel someone standing behind. It was Jay and Gita. They gave a smile and sat beside Partha, as Gita put her hand around Partha's neck.

Partha felt that she had to speak something. 'Look, I know it's selfish of me. You got your mother. But I am getting a sense of unfairness. You know what I mean?' she said this in quite a weak tone. 'Don't take it the wrong way.'

'What about the years we lived without her?' asked Gita.

Partha looked up at the face of Gita, but didn't say anything.

'Your mother's alright ... for sure,' said Jay, quite comfortingly.

'I really do hope so,' replied Partha.

The three didn't have much to talk about. They had better start focusing on what was going to happen in their journey. Who was guarding the book? The mystery was left unsolved. People had said only the Thunder bloodline knew what or who was guarding the book, but it remained a legacy secret. Some say it is a monster, but the three were wondering what bigger monster would be than the ones they had crossed already. Some say it is an unsolvable charm, which sounds true, as they hadn't yet met with any kind of dangerous illusion nor trick yet. But whatever was lingering in the dark, they were ready to face it.

Jay decided to break the ice with a vital question. 'So ... when are we leaving?'

'Well, we have to leave tomorrow morning. We don't have any choice,' replied Partha.

'But what about mom and Brej?'

'We would meet them after we get the book.'

'Don't be so optimistic,' interrupted Partha. 'Going in and returning alive from the *Land of Phantoms* is not so simple.'

'What makes you say that?' asked Jay, almost sarcastically.

Gita and Partha looked at Jay like he was out of his mind.

'Hey! What's wrong if I show some optimism once in a while?'

Gita simply ignored Jay. 'Why don't we take Brej and mom with us?'

'You want them to die for you? A life has already been sacrificed for you! Do you want two more to go like that? And all the more, a quest started by someone should be finished by themselves.'

Gita didn't have a suitable response for this. What Partha had told now was practical. Not only her, but everyone wouldn't be able to bear it if another life had been destroyed. Now it has been confirmed. It was the only three for the rest of the quest, and no one else.

'Well it's almost dawn,' Jay said.

'Time really flies fast here,' added Gita.

'Guess we have to get some sleep.'

Jay and Gita went inside the cave, and Partha, with one last glance at the sky which was slowly brightening, joined them guessing that this was going to be the last time the three were going to have a good *sleep*.

***

Az, Bingo and the three little cousins had almost reached the entry of the castle. Now, they were wondering how they were going to cross the giant lake once more. They were thinking about a good idea, as they didn't have Jay's sword which he had helped them last time. The lake had evaporated near the banks, and there was one huge rock connecting from the lake to the bank on the other side. But how were they going to cross the water without Jay's sword? The cousins had also turned serious, and were thinking of a good idea. They could see one giant tree leaning on one side, almost uprooted, as Sara came up with an idea. She thought once more, and thought if there was an easier way, but it looked like there was nothing else. It was morning, and there were no Scelps or sorcerers near, except one old sorcerer who looked loony. She went towards Az and asked: 'Where are the guards?'

'Guards ... oh you mean the Scelps ... They must have gone for a break.'

'Break? At this time?'

'This is the only time in the whole day. The crack of dawn. The law says that for half an hour, exactly thirty minutes, the Scelps are allowed to take a break. But after that, there are no breaks, holidays, nothing except these thirty minutes.'

'Wow. I think everyone would like to take that job.' muttered Arjun. 'It must be *so* fun.'

Sara grimaced at Arjun. 'Anyway, I have an idea.'

'What?'

'You see that tree? Up there? The tall-almost-uprooted one?'

'Yeah ... but what's that to do with crossing the lake kid?'

'Listen. We need power. Just power. Do you know anything that has power?'

'I may know,' said Bingo. He whistled as loud as he could as the sound echoed thrice. Nothing had happened for a few seconds as they could hear loud flaps of wings. They looked around in dismay, as the cousins erupted with joy.

'Polskite!' shouted Arjun.

'Yes!' shouted Sara. 'But ... he has got friends! Polskite's got friends! Look!' She pointed at Polskite, with five other griffins following him. The other one was quite bigger than Polskite, while the other was a little smaller, and the remaining three almost the same size as him.

The pride of griffins landed down to the ground as the cousins ran and hopped on Polskite.
'Nice!' exclaimed Az.
'Yeah ... I will tell you my plan. First, we tell Polskite to knock that tree down,' Sara started.
'Knock that tree?'
'Yes. If we knock down that tree straight down, it would fall between where we are standing to the rock out there. So, we should do nothing except walk on the tree to reach the other side. We have to also do it before the creatures in the lake munch the wood off. We will have only some time.'
'Sounds tough,' said Bingo.
'Also sounds the only way,' added Az. 'And the wood of these trees are extremely hard to break. But even with that, we only have some time. The creatures here can chop the wood like a piranha.'

Bingo jogged down to Polskite and explained the plan. The creature should have understood, if not, it would be too late. The others were praying for the tree to fall correctly, and they could cross the lake.
'Three! Two! One!' Bingo yelled as Polskite bolted towards the tree. He bumped straight to the tree as the whole bark vibrated. Slowly, roots started to pull off, but it was of no use. Polskite tried once more. There was no change except that the tree was leaning to the other side. Polskite raced down again as the tree started to shake. With a great thud, it crashed to the rock as they expected. It sounded like a plane crashing on a rocky airport, and they knew they had to

cross it fast or the creatures were going to eat their bridge…or worse the Scelps would come.

Az and Bingo led the line to cross the lake. Polskite and her entire pride flew off to the other side in an instant. It was very simple for them. But for Bingo, Az and the cousins ... *eh*, not so much.

Bingo slowly placed his shivering legs on the tree trunk. The creatures present in the river were looking at him, waiting for a nice breakfast but they weren't biting the wood yet.

As Bingo made his first couple of steps, Az joined him too. They were both trying to balance on the trunk as if they were tightrope walkers.

Az looked down at the hungry creatures. They still didn't seem to figure out that they could just bite the wood. 'Don't look down. Just don't.'

'Thanks,' muttered Bingo.

Nevertheless, he took Az's advice and moved on. Now, the cousins too got on the trunk and balanced themselves quite neatly.

After a minute of two, the wood was becoming a bit slippery. The five found it pretty hard to balance themselves and had some pretty close calls.

Tara missed her footing and almost fell into the water. Thankfully, her hands got hold of the log in a crawling position. She precariously got up and started walking again. She was pretty rattled by that.

'Phew! That was close.'

The wood started to screech. The trunk was narrowing every step and now everyone had to be even more attentive. Bingo took another step when he slipped. He was about to fall down as Az pulled him up. They saw that they had at least two hundred to three hundred metres to cross. Suddenly, something unexpected happened. The creatures in the water who were helplessly waiting started chomping on the wood. They had figured it out. This couldn't have come at a worse time. The wood had started to crack in some places and was looking seriously unstable. They had reached the intersection of the branches of the tree as well.

'Everyone! Walk as fast as you can!' yelled Az. 'The wood is cracking!'

Everyone started walking as fast as they could, and it was absolutely difficult. The wood produced larger and larger cracks. It looked like the wood was going to break into pieces any time now. Bingo, followed by the cousins and Az, one behind each other, walked as fast as they could on the relatively thin branches of the tree. Suddenly, a large crack was heard. The creatures had chopped off a large part of the trunk. Three-fourth of the tree was gone. Now the branches had been fully cracked. Az couldn't walk or even move without the risk of the branch giving away.

'Az! Az!' Everyone shouted in chorus.

But shouting was not going to do any help. The part on which Az was about to step had floated away. Now Az had to make a decision. Bingo reached for Az, but his hand was not long enough. Az gave a cold smile, as he threw his bow and his quiver to Bingo, who understood what Az was about to do.

'NO! You cannot do this!' he shouted, as the three cousins noticed one old sorcerer in the sky floating towards them. Az, with a calm face, jumped down to the water. He was struggling to swim due to the current and ripples the creatures created. One large crocodile with the teeth of a piranha spotted Az. It started swimming ferociously towards him. Az saw the creature and started moving his hands and legs vigorously towards the shore where Bingo was readily holding his hand out. Az reached for Bingo and fortunately for him, he caught Bingo's hand. As he felt Az's grip, he immediately pulled him back up as the creature opened and shut its mouth, expecting Az's body to be within its grasp. But now, they had a new issue. The sorcerer was heading closer and they could hear his cunning laughter as they longed for a victim for Thunder. He had to protect the cousins right now. He was thinking of a good idea to knock the old man out when Sara got one.

'UNCLE BINGO! THE BOW AND ARROWS!' she shouted.

'Wh- What? No way!' Bingo shouted back. The cousins ran towards him as fast as Sara snatched the bow from Bingo. There was a quiver full of arrows. She picked three arrows and put two of them on the ground, with one in her hand for firing. She really didn't have any knowledge of using a bow, but she had seen Gita practice a few times. She tried her best to aim at the man who was running and shot the arrow! The arrow went straight and pierced the stomach of the old sorcerer who was surprised to see him getting attacked by a little girl and opened his toothless mouth. He slowly started to turn dizzy and fell down into the river. The creatures who were circling the trunk in hunger were gleeful that at least they had got a little meat. They chomped the man to nothingness in less than a second.

'Whoo!' shouted Tara. 'That was cool!'

Bingo was quite shell-shocked and so was Sara. They couldn't believe that Sara's aim was that precise.

Suddenly Tara changed the topic. 'Az! What about him?' she pointed at Az gasping for breath, lying a few metres away from them. They ran towards Az and saw that he was totally wet, with a cut near the shoulder of his right hand. It was not that deep but it still should have hurt. His hair was dropped to one side due to its wetness but otherwise, he looked fine. His clothes were soaked and one part of it was slightly torn. He started spitting water and recovering as Sara yelled:

'RUN! RUN!'

Bingo looked to the other side and noticed that the sorcerers were just out of the break and were bolting towards the lake. The sorcerers were at least five hundred metres away from them. The best they could do was hide. Bingo pulled the hand of Az, who was only half-conscious. The cousins started running, trying to find a suitable place to hide. Poor Bingo was putting his hands around the shoulder of Az, and was almost carrying him. Az's energy had drained a significant amount.

'Man! You're heavy!' commented Bingo.

They ran as fast as they could, as Tara noticed a huge rock which was large enough to hide them. 'THERE!' she yelled.

Bingo finally went behind the rock. He slowly let Az sit down, who was panting and coughing badly.

'Thank you,' he said to Bingo.

'Well that was a little difficult,' Bingo replied, panting.

Sara slowly peeked up the rock and noticed the crowd of sorcerers rampaging towards the uprooted bark.

The bewildered faces were clueless about what had happened. Many started fighting with each other, as the new head witch of the Scelps, and the head sorcerer stepped forward, deeply examining what had happened. Then a grin arose on the two evil faces. The head sorcerer knelt down leisurely and felt a footprint of a shoe. It was surely the footprint of Bingo. Later, the head witch pointed at numerous footprints leading straight down to the place in which they were hiding. These footprints were tinier and quite blatantly, it was of the three little cousins. The entire gang understood as a cheeky grin sprouted on their faces.

'Uh oh. They've found out,' said Arjun, noticing the witches and sorcerers from the side.

'We have to run! Everyone! To the castle!' Sara said, slightly whispering.

They were lucky that Az had turned conscious, as they started racing towards the castle back door without any hesitation.

'THERE THEY ARE!' A witch yelled.

'GO TO THE BACK DOOR!' yelled Sara.

'I don't think so,' replied Bingo, pointing at the back entrance of the castle.

They were *shocked.* There were at least fifty witches flooding the back door too! Actually, even Az didn't know that Thunder had hired such great numbers of sorcerers and witches. Now they were trapped. They were surrounded by witches all around. There were cunning laughs of witches and sorcerers all sound, but there was no escape. Sara crumpled her brain to think of a good idea, but her brain had run out. The huge crowd of witches and sorcerers from the other side had also appeared. From the huge crowd of sorcerers emerged the head witch, who was more wicked than Advillsia, the head witch they had seen getting fired by Thunder last time.

'Oh so *look* who it is!' the head witch said in a bossy voice, circling the five.

'The old watchman!' the crowd started whispering into each other's ears.

'Can I know the reason why you are here? Anyway you wouldn't live for supper tonight ... that is for sure ...' she said, still moving around the five.

'Look, you can do anything you want to me, but spare that man and the kids,' said Az.

'Well ... isn't that *unfair*? They are visitors too ... and all the more they are humans! I can smell the blood!'

'They are humans but they know about Olympia.'

'Oh I pity you…for bringing humans to Olympia. Now or later, you would be torn into pieces.'

The head witch stood straight towards Sara, and touched her cheeks. The witch saw the cousins' frightened faces. She moved towards Sara. 'Oh ... what a cute little girl you are! But… I am afraid that you won't be alive,' she said in a low voice.

Bingo whispered to the cousins. 'Get out of here. Now. Save yourselves.'

'Aww…How sweet…' the witch mused. 'All in vain, though.'

The others started chanting the witch's name as she gave a smirk of pure evil at the five. She walked a couple of steps back, as she got her hands together. Bingo, Az and the cousins were quite frightened and had no idea what was going to happen next. Along with the continuous chant of 'DIE! DIE!' it seemed a lot more terrifying. Slowly, a ball of bright blue fire started to form within the hands of the witch. The dangerous fire was reflected into the appalled eyes of Bingo and the others, as the cousins forced their eyes shut. The other witches backed off, and the five could feel the heat. The ball of fire grew bigger and bigger so did the grins of the witches. The witch was about to force the ball of fire into the five when there was a *flash!* Someone had cast a counter curse to the wicked witch as her fireball faded into ashes.

~CHAPTER TEN~

Ostragon Trouble

Jay, Partha and Gita had hardly slept. They had spent almost the whole night planning about what they had to do next. Asha and Brej woke up early and took a quiet walk outside the cave. The atmosphere around the cave was pretty decent, with the pretty lush bushes of water-berries growing and some faded grass here and there also could be found.

After they finished their walk, they came into the cave and woke Jay, Gita and Partha up.

'Wake up, kids! yelled Brej.

Jay slowly got up and stretched himself. Gita and he had slept, supporting their backs on a rock, and it looked as if Partha had never slept. Asha smiled at Jay and gave a hand to him. He had dark circles under his eyes and didn't want to proceed with the quest after having such a rough night. But Partha was yet determined, and was scaling the distance from the cave and the darkest portion. The sky was already a hue of blood red, which made everything look darker, but they knew that the weather and the sky would turn darker and more dangerous. They didn't know if Brej and Asha still knew that they were going to leave the cave soon, but Gita and Jay surely felt harsh to say that. After all, they had only seen their mother for the first time! Jay was comforting himself by stuffing a few fruits and drinking a lot of water, as the normal food seemed a feast to him.

'Jay, calm down!' said Asha. 'You are going to choke!'

'Don't worry, I'm sure choking won't be the worst thing which will happen in this land.'

Gita was munching on a small packet of stale biscuits which she had managed to bring from earth. Though it tasted really bad, she had to somehow fill her ravenous stomach.

Asha took the bowl Jay was eating in and threw in the makeshift sink, which was really just a hole made of clay. 'So ... is your dad still-'

Jay suddenly got a reminder. 'Dad! Az! They would have reached the castle now wouldn't they?'

'They should have,' said Gita.

'And you guys are staying here for sure aren't you?' asked Asha.

There was a sudden silence. Partha, who was looking out, turned swiftly as Jay swallowed the fruits. Gita looked as pale as ever and no one knew what answer they had to give.

'Ah…well… mom…we cannot leave a quest which we started…just like that,' managed Jay.

'No way you are continuing this are you?' asked Asha

'But ma, the whole planet is depending on us! Including earth!' said Gita.

'But you guys are just kids! I cannot leave my children to get into trouble!'

'Please mom! You cannot leave millions of people to die!'

'Please understand, my children. I want you safe.'

'I get it,' said Jay. 'But this is important for the lives of many people.'

'Fine…'

'Yes, thank you!' shouted Gita.

'But with one condition,' said Asha.

'What is it?'

'I am *coming* with you.'

'What?' the three shouted together.

'Bu-but no

'If you want to go, I am coming with you.'

'Mom, that would be more dangerous than ever. Dad trusted us to come here ... why can't you?' said Jay.

'I am coming with you and that is final.'

Brej finally spoke up. 'Asha, you cannot do that.' 'A quest started by someone should be finished by themselves. They are in this quest for some reason. Not only to get the *Enchanted Book Of Resurrection.* Either stopping them, or accompanying them will only lead to the worst.'

'BREJ! Have you lost your sense! They can't ... they need help!'

'Whatever you say, that is true,' said Brej. 'But you will only be putting them in danger.'

'Ok. Fine.' Slowly, a smile arose on three faces of Jay, Gita, and Partha.

'But promise me one thing. Promise that you would return safely. Promise that you would see me again. Promise that you *all* would come *alive*. I don't want *anyone* to die.'

'We promise,' the three said in chorus though they were too not fully confident. But, ever since their mom was found alive, Jay and Gita had a boost of confidence. Jay and Gita hugged their mom as she shed a tear. Partha and Brej smiled.

They just took one last look at the cave and planned to head out. Jay and Gita hugged their mom, hopefully not for the last time and so did Partha. Asha and Brej wished them good luck as the three went off as Jay, Gita and Partha stepped out of the cave to continue their quest. After a couple of minutes, Asha and Brej looked like mere ants waving. The three took one last look, waved in return and walked on as their faces totally vanished. There was an awkward silence for the first couple of minutes as Jay and Gita were thinking if it was a bad idea to leave their mom there itself but then again they didn't want their mom to face such dangers as themselves. Anyway, she was considered dead with one of Thunder's ex-board members for fifteen years. Jay and Gita needed to collect the fact that she was alive.

Partha broke the silence by asking a very straightforward question.

'So ... where do we go now?'

The others suddenly realised that they had been strolling pointlessly towards nowhere.

'Uhh ...' fumbled Jay. 'I ... don't exactly know.'

Gita shrugged in reply.

Partha pointed towards a direction which smelled more horrible and disgusting. 'Well ... this way looks promising.'

'I don't get your definition of "*promising*" but ... fine.'

So, they started their march towards the cluster of grey clouds which had bolts of lightning slashing once in a while. It was really tough to get going after the incident that had unfolded, but they had no choice.

'Isn't there any way we can reach there fast?' asked Jay.

'I don't think so,' Gita said in a low voice.

'Well I guess there is,' Partha replied with a gentle smile on her face. She wiped the sweat off her forehead and knelt down, putting her finger into the mud.

'What are you doing?' Gita asked, looking at Partha's actions.

'*Ostragons*,' replied Partha.

Jay was perplexed. 'What?'

'Their scent,' replied Partha, ignoring Jay's question, which puzzled Jay and Gita more.

'Scent? What are you talking about?' Jay asked.

'Wait a minute, will you? said Partha, putting her hand into the sand. Then, she picked up a huge pile and took it towards her nose. She sniffed it like a dog, as she opened her eyes wide open.

'North!' she yelled.

'Hey, will you stop spitting out words and tell me what you are talking about?' asked Jay

'Shh…' said Partha. '*Ostragons.* They are one of the most commonly found creatures in the Equatorial region of Olympia. They usually live in huge flocks, and are known for their sensitiveness to even the tiniest sounds. Understood? *Now* follow me.'

'Did you just swallow the encyclopaedia?' asked Gita.

'It is just like you guys studied about tigers and lions on your planet,' replied Partha.

'Okay. That's fair.'

'I have a question for you,' asked Gita to Partha. 'Have you ever gone to school? Or ... whatever you call it ... Penplas or something?'

Partha frowned. 'No. But my dad taught me some things and most of it was learned by myself out of my own interest.'

'Well ... so how are these creatures going to help us?' asked Jay.

'They carry us of course.'

Carry? Jay was thinking. *Are those of the size of horses? Donkeys? Elephants?*

Anyway, he decided to carry on, and left all the guiding stuff to Partha.

'So, we follow the scent,' she replied.

'Well, we are not dogs are we?'

'Their scent is strong enough that even we can smell them,' replied Partha. 'Anyway, for now, follow my lead.'

Partha slowly started walking, following the scent of the Ostragons. Jay and Gita still couldn't smell it, but they didn't know why. But they saw that it was better for them to just leave it and follow Partha.

'You really can smell it?' asked Jay in surprise.

'Can you?' Partha asked with a scowl.

'Of course ... Of course!' lied Jay.

They were moving in the northern direction, which was also the direction on which the entry of the Land Of Phantoms was located. Slowly, the scent started to turn stronger. Though it was still feeble for Jay and Gita, they could yet smell it a bit. They started to move faster and faster, and now the scent was getting quite strong. The scent smelled mostly of wet clay with a tinge of wet socks like the creatures hadn't taken a bath in quite a long time. Nevertheless, they kept following Partha, wondering if it was the right direction. But now, Jay and Gita felt sure that they were getting closer as the smell started to get very strong. But Partha kept on walking. Suddenly, a blurred vision was seen in the distance.

Partha had a pleased look on her face. 'Look, there come the Ostragons.'

Jay and Gita couldn't see them at first but they became more and more visible as they ran as fast as a cheetah leaving a cloud of dust behind them. Their speed looked to be slowly slowing down as they neared the three. They could clearly see the features of the Ostragons now.

Jay sighed in disappointment. 'Oh! Come on! All that "*most important creature in Olympia*" was just for a lame ostrich?'

Partha was perplexed. 'Ostrich?'

'Ostriches are flightless birds who run around very fast and lay mammoth eggs and they smell like gym socks.'

'Very detailed explanation, Jay,' mumbled Gita.

Even though the Ostragons had slowed down, they were still running as fast as a ... well ... ostrich. Their features were getting more and more clear. They had a body covered with soft, orange feathers. Even the neck was covered with a few feathers but they were a bit lighter. It had a sharp pointy, yellow coloured beak which was perfect for eating branches and whatever else they could find.

Other than that, their features were pretty similar to that of a regular ostrich back on Earth. There were many young ones in the flock too running at the same speed. The flock looked quite organised and was running in stunning synchronicity. Jay, Gita and Partha stopped walking to avoid any more sudden movements.

Partha signalled the others to bend down. Jay and Gita were confused but agreed.

'Now, remember. NO SUDDEN MOVEMENTS OR SOUNDS. Ostragons are extremely sound sensitive,' whispered Jay.

'I don't know why we have to talk like we are discussing the team strategies in a football match,' complained Jay.

'Because ... as I said-'

'Yeah. Yeah. I heard what you said,' interrupted Jay.

Partha scowled at Jay as she got up from crouching.

'Wait,' said Gita, having a thought in her mind. 'Why are we doing this? Why can't we just turn to the other side or go sideways?'

Jay agreed. 'Yeah, you may have a point. Why are we doing this?'

Both of them looked at Partha.

Partha sighed. *Must I explain everything?* She thought. 'We are doing this because we need a mode of transportation. We can't possibly walk the whole way.'

'Why? Are we really that far?' asked Jay.

'Jay. You might have not noticed yet, but this place is huge!'

The Ostragons had now stopped about a couple of metres away from them.

'Let's go!' whispered Partha.

She started tip-toeing toward the Ostragons. Jay and Gita followed her. She was slowly moving towards one particular Ostragon who was munching on some dry twigs on the ground. It had an exceptionally feathery body, perfect for sitting on during a ride. Jay saw Partha's actions and started moving towards the other side of the Ostragon. Gita went in between Jay and Partha. The Ostragon was at the very front of the flock and all the others were at the back. Just as Jay was about to step on the back of the creature, another Ostragon saw their movements and cawed in alarm. Hearing that signal, the other Ostragons started fleeing at a crazy speed. The Ostragon Jay, Gita and Partha were trying to get on, and started fleeing too. It was running even faster than the others.

Partha started running. 'Come on! We have to hitch a ride on these things!'

'How?' shouted Gita. 'They are moving too fast!'

'Run!'

The three started running at their maximum speed. But the Ostragons were moving too fast for the three to outrun. Just as the Ostragons from the back were about to trample Jay, Gita and Partha, Gita pushed Jay and Partha aside as the Ostragons ran right where they should have been.

Gita was panting. 'Guys! Be a little more careful out there! We were about to become Ostragon kill!'

Jay and Partha were too appalled and exhausted to respond.

Jay finally stopped panting. 'She's right. But now we have to get the Ostragons.'

Partha nodded.

'Fine ...' Gita said. 'But it's not my fault if we become Ostragon-kill.'

'Sounds fair enough.' Jay started running again. Gita and Partha followed. By now only a few Ostragons were in sight. But they were still running quite fast. The three were running with all their might. Suddenly they saw a steep cliff just a couple of hundred metres in front of them.

'Oh! Come on! A cliff? Seriously?' Jay exclaimed. 'This day is getting worse and worse.'

Gita and Partha understood what he meant. If there was a cliff Ostragons would have fallen down it and probably got seriously hurt. They surely cannot jump down those creatures which were running as fast as race cars, and at the same time, cross the cliff! The Ostragons surely cannot jump the cliff, as the other side was at least a two hundred metres far. Jay thought they had gone through enough dangers. The only thing which they hadn't yet experienced was falling down from a cliff which was 800 metres high. They had to grab on one Ostragon. Anyway, they were of no use! Just as they were bolting, they saw one Ostragon running beside them. This was their only luck.

'Gita! Partha! Look!' shouted Jay, as the three noticed the Ostragon.

'Quickly! Jump on it!' yelled Partha. Jay with the same momentum, took a sideways leap, grabbed the creature's feathery back and heaved himself on its back. He could barely believe that he managed to accomplish this but he knew it wasn't over.

'Gita! Your hand!' he yelled, as Gita tried her best to keep up with Jay and the Ostragon.

'Jay!' she cried, as he pulled Gita on the Ostragons back. The Ostragons started running faster and faster, so the distance between the cliff was reducing rapidly. Now it was only Partha. She was running as fast as she could, as Gita stretched her arm.

'Partha! Grab on!' she shouted. But it wasn't as easy as it sounded. The Ostragons were not creatures so easy to outrun. Though Partha wasn't a one who would easily give up. With all her might, she pushed herself forward. Now, there was only a hundred metre gap between them and the cliff. Now it was do or die for Partha.

'C'mon!' shouted Jay.

Partha had already started thinking horrible thoughts. *What if she was stranded here? What if she couldn't get on the Ostragon?*

But she still didn't lose confidence. She pushed and pushed and pushed. Finally, she jumped and caught Gita's hands. She leaped onto the back of the Ostragon and was relieved.

'You made it!' Jay shouted.

'Now ...' Gita pointed straight.

The cliff was not even fifty metres! Now they started to think.

'WAIT? We are about to crash down a huge cliff!' yelled Jay. 'How could we be this stupid?'

'There must be a reason these Ostragons are running towards that cliff!'

'There better be one!' replied Gita.

'AHHHHHHHHHHHH!' they yelled in chorus and shut their eyes in fear. Now, they could do literally nothing, except to trust their luck and all the more, trust the Ostragons. In a fraction of a second, they could feel a lame breeze tickling their face. They could smell some smoke, and coughed continuously. Now, they could confirm that they were at least alive, Jay peeked out with an eye, and could see nothing except a red, blood orange sky, with smoke all around. They were stunned. They were flying! They started smiling in excitement, but at the same time, they were speechless.

'OSTRAGONS CAN FLY?' Partha yelled. 'I honestly never knew that!'

'So that was the reason they were running towards the cliff! To migrate to the other side!' Gita discovered

'WHOA!' Jay said. 'Looks like you didn't swallow the whole encyclopaedia! Some bits were left out for sure.'

Partha scowled at Jay.

They weren't at a very tall height, though it was reasonable. They slowly saw the Ostragon they were seated on, and noticed a major difference. The Ostragon had sprouted wings! It had black scaly wings exactly like a dragon, and they could see a whole herd of them flying at front! All the Ostragons had similar wings, though the size mattered.

'So this gives them the name!' said Gita.

They could say that this was the only exciting part of their journey till now. Though it was a rough start, it was worth the effort. They could see the red, dusty sand, and a couple of boulders lying here and there, but still couldn't see what was down the cliff. A huge group of black clouds, which they had been following from the beginning looked larger. It was truly a wonderful view, but they had to understand what was behind it. More dangers, tasks, creatures, even things which they couldn't imagine.

~CHAPTER ELEVEN~

The Gateway Of Death

The three were really lucky. What would have happened if the Ostragons couldn't fly? What if they didn't even find the Ostragons? They would have been sitting in front of the cliff not knowing what to do. Anyway, destiny had taken them in the right path. Now, they had to do nothing except to proceed on their feet. Now, the other side of the cliff was lamely visible. The Ostragons were surprisingly fast in the air too, but not as fast as their speed on the ground. The Ostragon on which they were riding suddenly cawed in a piercingly loud voice, which scared them quite a bit, as another Ostragon cawed back (which they assumed to be a reply).

'Whoa!' Gita said in excitement.

'Unfortunately, there are no books which state the language of Ostragons.' mocked Jay.

Suddenly, even before Partha could reply, the Ostragons surprised them. They dropped lower and soared down, which scared the three quite a bit.

'WHAT HAPPENED?' asked Gita, a minute after the Ostragons settled at a lower height.

'They are communicating. Looks like we will reach soon,' said Partha. 'Wherever that is.'

The other side of the cliff was almost there. After flying for at least fifteen minutes, the Ostragons started to soar down slowly, dropping down in altitude. The creatures were smart enough, and glided down smoothly, knowing that a fast sly down would cause a dangerous crash. Finally, the Ostragons touched the ground with their muscular feet and started running like a plane which just landed. Slowly, the speed started to dwindle and they came to a halt.

'Uhh…' Jay sighed, feeling a little dizzy with the constant change in altitude.

The three waited patiently for the Ostragons to fully stop and settle, and didn't want them to start flying again.

Jay decided to get down first. He stroked the Ostragon for one last time, making sure that they don't fly off along with them like he did last time with the butterflies.

He made himself feel as light as he could and turned, hopping down to the ground slowly. Next was Partha. Jay gave one hand to her and she jumped down.

'I could have done that without you,' grunted Partha.

'Yeah, sure,' replied Jay.

Now it was only Gita. She was quite scared that the Ostragons might run off anytime. But ignoring her thoughts, she tried getting down like normally how she gets down on a bicycle. Unfortunately, it wasn't the same. The Ostragon was quite large and it was quite hard to get her other leg all the way from the other side. She somehow managed to do so and tried getting down. Jay tried lending her a hand. But before he could do so, a loud '*Crunch!*' was heard. Partha looked back and noticed that she stepped on a pile of charred, dry sticks.

Uh oh, she thought as the Ostragons started cranking up their engines, speeding through the charred ground. The other Ostragons too followed. Gita started screeching as she was holding the Ostragons folded wing and prayed for life that she wouldn't fall. The Ostragon got more and crankier as Gita held the wing. She was desperately trying to climb over the Ostragon so that she could sit more comfortably. Jay and Partha ran with all their might, trying to catch up. But obviously, it was of no use. They were shouting frantically for Gita but she couldn't hear them or even see them for that matter. Jay and Partha didn't have any choice except to run behind those Ostragons. The scenario looked exactly like a frantic cop running behind a criminal. The Ostragons started picking up speed, as Jay and Partha tried harder. Gita didn't know what to do. Surely, a fall from the Ostragon would cause a severe injury. She started looking around, perplexed, with her hair flying in all directions. She tried pulling out feathers from the Ostragon, though it looked as if it heated up the creature more. Jay and Partha, yelling Gita's name, had to come up with a plan, but they couldn't think of any, especially in a time when their friend is dragged down to death.

'What should we do!' shouted Jay.

'As if I set the Ostragons on her!' Partha shouted back.

'JAY! JAY!' Gita was yelling, but they wondered, where will the Ostragons stop?

After chasing for at least a couple of miles, they slowed down and halted. Gita jumped from the Ostragon and fell to the ground, which was quite an impact. She was coughing and panting for the first few minutes, and got up. Partha and Jay ran to Gita and knelt down, and were shocked. In front of them was flowing a *river,* a river made of some smouldering lava with venomous flame emitting.

'Oh no,' said Partha. 'It seems like we have come across the *Gateway Of Death.*'

~CHAPTER THIRTEEN ~

A Strange Guide

In the meanwhile, Earth hadn't calmed down even a bit. As always, the mystery had spread all across the world, and it had turned to be a world issue. While some countries started blaming each other, some decided not to get involved in such an issue. At such a modern time like this, it was really rare for murders such as this to happen, especially in such a highly protected area. The CCTVs were surely useful, but in this case, humans had to find out the truth on their own. Still, the detectives were searching like vultures, though they still didn't get a single clue. The press had also been pressuring for the police to spit out the truth, but the truth was that the government themselves didn't have a clue. Well, the rumour about Stoming related to the recent murders had come to an end, though his name had popped out in several news channels. But today, there was a shocking discovery. A clever detective had compared the thumb-print imprinted on a shelf with the one of Stoming, and came to a conclusion that Stoming wasn't the one. Since Stoming was the only suspect kept in the minds of almost everyone, The FBI decided to cover it up to not confuse the locals.

***

With wide and bewitched eyes, shocked, the three moved near the *gateway of Death*. You may wonder, a gateway of Death? Is the entrance to the middle of The Land Of Phantoms some kind of barbed wire? Or perhaps an electric gate? Well, of course not. But this was surely dangerous. They felt a sudden rise in the temperature, which made them sweat frantically. The ground was also hot, and the ground seemed as if it was just an inch from a volcano which was about to explode. There was thick, black ash bolting towards the faces of the three, as they started coughing rapidly. I am sure, no one can surely stand such heat for more than an hour. Now, the only doubt for you would be what is the gateway of Death? It is a River of Flames. A dense, flowing, river of green and blood red lava, with hot, sparkling flames shooting out of it. The scariest thing was the red bubbles of lava oozing out.

'Well, I didn't expect that,' said Jay, his face pale, both from the heat and the shock.

'Neither did I,' replied Gita, with her eyes fixed on the river.

'The River of Flames! I have read about it!' yelled Partha with a bright face.

'What haven't you read about?' mocked Jay.

Suddenly, a mysterious force attracted her towards the river. Though she knew it was the most dangerous thing in the whole universe, she couldn't avoid walking towards it. In fact, she had almost forgotten about Jay and Gita, how they had crossed all the obstacles, almost everything! To say in short words, she was totally mesmerised by the river. The two noticed Gita walking towards the river, and immediately ran behind her.

'GITA! ARE YOU MAD?'

Jay blocked Gita's view and Partha pulled her behind with a great force, as Gita fell behind.

'Wh-What…happened?' she asked, dazed.

'What happened? You just ran towards the river which was about to melt you! *What happened,* you ask!' yelled Jay.

'JAY! Stop yelling at her! There is no mistake at her side! It happens to everyone! Even you, if you keep looking at it!'

'*When to the river,*
your eyes are anchored
You will forget it is the greatest fear,
To the door of your death you will canter,' narrated Partha.

'Do you think the river is an illusion?' asked Gita.

'Well…there is a slight chance. Let me test it out,' replied Partha.

She stepped towards Jay and grabbed his sword. The sword still looked bright and majestic, as Jay used to polish it every single day. Surely, having the most powerful sword of the whole time was an honour, and there was no doubt Jay was the one who had to have it. She looked at the clean blade and felt it, with her wide eyes fixed on the 'F' carved in the handle.

'HEY! That's my sword there!' yelled Jay, not expecting Partha to grab his sword.

She didn't hear the words of Jay, but slowly started to walk near the river. This time, she was more focused, and didn't even look at the sparkling flames. She felt like she was being roasted in an oven and could also sense the spirit of the river attempting to hypnotize her. With full concentration, she took the tip of the blade and drenched Jay's sword into the river.

'What do you think you are doing?' Jay yelled and ran towards Partha. But it was too late. She had already dropped the sword into the river as it totally melted in.

'WHY WOULD YOU THAT?' shouted Jay.

'Don't worry,' replied Partha calmly. 'The sword of Frencher is the most powerful sword. Nothing can destroy it.'

'Then what did I see now?' asked Jay, trying to calm himself a bit.

'To my eyes, it looked like his sword was drenched in a river of lava and got broken down to piec-' Just before Gita could finish her sentence, something surprised them. A blue light slowly took the shape of Jay's sword and rested on his hands.

'Cool!' Jay shouted in joy.

In a matter of a second, all their faces turned serious.

'So, this is not an illusion. If the river could burn down the Frencher's sword, it is surely dangerous,' concluded Partha.

'Then, how are we going to cross this?' asked Jay with a pale face.

'Maybe, we can look for its start and move around it,' suggested Jay.

'Impossible,' replied Partha.

'This river is the longest in the world. It is just a tributary of the river of Poison back at Olympia.'

Suddenly, Gita felt something awkward. She felt like something was calling her. She slowly peeked into the small, ragged bag, which she had got from the cave where they met their mother. Inside, she saw a small, warm gleam around the map. She took the map out, and uncurled it. She was shocked.

'Guys! Look at this!'

Jay and Partha ran up to her.

They took a deep look at the map, and were stunned. Slowly, words were starting to appear own their own. It looked to be the same handwriting they had seen on the piece of parchment they had seen the last time, and was written in pitch-black ink. The slanting handwriting was slightly difficult to read, though it was readable.

Finally, all the words had appeared.

Jay slowly took the map from Gita and read:

'You may be awestruck,
Wondering where to go,
Begging for good luck,
You would be wandering to and fro.
Wait there, I would say,
It still is your day.
A guide will lead you,
But you will have a gift to pay,
Tall and thin,
Soaring around with a body of translucent blue
Wait there, wait till he comes to you.'

'Ok…' said Jay. 'It is mentioning a guide of some sort.'

'Yeah,' replied Gita. 'It is also mentioning the guide having a body of translucent blue. So…a ghost? Or are there any other creatures we don't know about?' She looked at Partha, expecting a comment from her.

Partha read it a couple of times to understand it. 'No, but that doesn't make sense. Why would a ghost help us?'

'Maybe it's a nice one.'

'Let me read it once more.'

'You may be awestruck,
wondering where to go
Begging for good luck,
you would be wandering to and fro.'

'Sounds similar,' said Partha with a little chuckle.

'Wait there, I would say,
It still is your day.
A guide will lead you,'

'It is asking us to wait here,' said Jay.

'Yes, yes, stop stating the obvious,' replied Partha hastily.

'But you will have a gift to pay,'

'A gift? What kind of a gift?' asked Gita.
'It might be a gift that the guide would demand,' said Jay.
'Mmm…could be.'
Partha continued reading.

'Tall and thin,
Soaring around with a body of translucent blue
Wait there, Wait there, wait till he comes to you.'

Gita still stood beside her original statement. 'A body of translucent blue…which is a ghost.'
'No, it can't be,' said Partha.
'How? It's the only logical explanation.'
'No, you don't get it, the ghosts in the Land Of The Phantoms are mostly tied to their king. They are not normally friendly to any visito-'
Before she could even finish his sentence, the three heard an eerie sound. They got a cold feeling as chills ran down their spine. They felt a sudden change in the temperature as though someone had turned on the AC. They felt some winds gushing through their faces and making a creepy noise which only added to the eerie atmosphere. They heard whoosh behind them, as Jay turned back, panting.
'Everyone, don't panic.'

As the three turned behind, they heard whoosh in front of them. The three were absolutely terrified even though they didn't show it. *What could this be? Could it be another vile, unknown creature lurking in the eerie spaces of the Land Of The Phantoms or could it be the mysterious guide?* These were just a few of the questions running rapidly in the minds of the three.

Now, it was getting creepier. Jay stood attentive, along with his sword, facing one direction, while Partha and Gita had loaded their arrows and waited for any sudden moment. Their hearts could be heard beating frantically. Slowly, they felt something nearing them. There was no sound of footsteps as the creepy noise intensified. It intensified to a point that they were certain that there was someone behind them. They turned around, weapons locked and loaded when they saw the creature. There was a tall, translucent figure, with a tinge of light blue. It was a ghost! Its face was as pale as they expected, and had faces exactly like humans, not even a bit scarier, though totally translucent. Till its hip, everything was translucent, and looked exactly like humans. But from the hip downwards, there was only blue-white smoke. The three had their terrified eyes shut and dared to look at the ghost. Jay had slashed through the ghost with his sword, though there was no harm caused. He slowly opened his eyes and so did the girls.

'Who are you?' asked Jay, still grasping his sword.

'Can't you see?' the ghost hissed in a creepy tone. While it talked, he could see a row full of dirty translucent teeth, and chains dangling down from both of its hands. Its voice sounded extremely eerie. Suddenly, it all stopped.

'Well, well, well, you didn't think that that was my real voice, did you?' the ghost asked, but this time, in a normal, humanly tone.

'Well, you must be our 'guide',' said Gita, hiding her fear quite brilliantly.

'First tell us who you are,' said Partha, joining Gita.

'Oh ... just call me Natt. I am a ghost, or a soul, or a phantom, or whatever we are called nowadays,' the ghost replied. He looked at Gita. 'Aren't you quite the charm? Yes it would be my pleasure to guide you, since you asked so nicely.'

'Excuse us for a moment,' said Partha and quickly pushed the other two into a small huddle.

'Okay…' replied Natt.

'Let me tell you,' started Partha, trying her best to keep her voice as calm as possible. 'This guy…err… ghost can't be trusted. As I said, they work for an evil force. Why would he be willing to help us?'

'It's true,' replied Gita. 'We can use the map.' She took the map out of her pocket to see it just as something unexpected happened. The map disintegrated right in her hands! The remains flew away with the wind. The three were flabbergasted.

'What was that?' asked Jay, not believing his eyes.

'I don't know,' replied Gita. 'But I guess we have no choice now but to follow the ghost.

'I don't know,' said Partha. 'I have a bad feeling about him.'

'Then you say you will carry on on your own, do you?' asked a voice from behind. It was Natt.

'How did you-'

'Well, here are a few tips. There are ghosts, creatures, and why, even insects waiting out there to gobble you ... and somehow if you cross them, by sheer dumb luck, you will have to meet something no living Olympian has never met before. Concluding, without my guidance, you will be dead even before you realise it.

The three formed a huddle again.

'Okay can we talk more softly?' asked Jay. 'That creep can hear us easily.'

'Okay, I think we can try following the ghost,' affirmed Gita. 'I mean ... it's not like we have any other option right?'

'Yes,' agreed Jay.

'I'm not sure about this but ... fine,' said Partha.

She turned Natt and nodded her head.

Natt did nothing but smile.

Meanwhile, Jay wasted no time. 'Okay, now...how are we supposed to cross this thing?' He pointed at the hot, oozing River Of Flames.

'You don't think that is so easy, do you?' said Natt.

'No, I don't. Which is why I am asking you.'

'Fair point. But first, I am going to need something from you.' Natt put his hand out.

At first, the three were confused but then they understood.

'The gift!' Partha cried out.

'You bet that's what I want,' replied Natt. 'I need something in return.'

'Anything?' asked Jay.

'Yup. Anything. Anything you got on the way.'

'*Anything* that we got?'

'Yes, *Anything*,' stressed Natt.

The three didn't know what to give him. They hadn't got anything on the way except ... getting tired by chasing the Ostragons, jumping lava puddles, escaping The Vulture Of flames. The only good thing they got was meeting Jay and Gita's mom, though they had to leave soon and didn't get the chance to spend much time with her.

Jay started to think. He had to give something to proceed further. He suddenly got an idea. 'Wait! I think I know what to give him!'

'What is it?' asked Gita.

'The leaf!'

'Wait…do you mean the leaf Gignos gave us?' asked Gita.

'Yes, we could use that,' replied Partha. Either way, I don't think anything else is there.'

'But still, Gignos gave that leaf to us, right?' asked Gita. 'I'm sure he wouldn't want us to give it to some stranger-ghost whom we met in the most terrifying place in Olympia.'

'Well, he could have given it for this too,' replied Jay. 'He said, "Consequences will teach you."'

'Yeah, but are you sure?'

'We have no choice.'

'Fine,' agreed Gita. 'Give him the leaf.'

Jay gently took the leaf from a small locket in his pocket. He slowly opened the locket and took the leaf to the ghost, as Natt took it slowly.

He looked a bit taken aback but didn't react much more. 'Very well.'

After he said this, bright, yellow light appeared as the leaf vanished into the body of the ghost.

~CHAPTER FOURTEEN~

Into The Heart

'Now, what are we supposed to do?' asked Jay.

'Follow me,' said Natt in a very mysterious voice. By the time the conversation was over, the three had forgotten the main reason they were talking to the ghost. Their bodies felt surprisingly hotter. Gita felt the temperature rise in her body.

'Guys, I don't feel so well,' said Gita, touching her forehead.

'Yes, I feel a bit hot too,' said Jay.

'That's because we are standing here so long,' replied Natt. 'Well, in my case, floating.'

'Can we get a move on here?' asked Partha, impatiently.

He started floating toward the bubbling molten river, and started mumbling something to himself. When Partha was about to move forward, he indicated to her to back off. After at least two minutes of chanting, he turned back and sprinkled something on the head of Gita. It looked shiny, and immediately vanished the second it touched Gita's head.

'What was that?'

'A pinch of *emparon dust.* A lot may be dangerous, even may be fatal. But small quantities may surely be useful,' replied Natt.

He walked towards Jay and Partha and sprinkled some dust, and said,

'Walk towards the fire.'

'What! Are you crazy!' cried Gita.

'No. Believe me. I've seen crazy.'

Gita hesitated a bit but started walking towards the fire.

Jay and Partha were appalled. 'Gita! Don't do that! It's a trap!'

But Gita ignored them and kept on walking. But she was praying to herself, totally frightened. How *could* she trust a pinch of dust, whatever its name might be and walk into a river full of hot flames and venom?

She felt hotter than ever as she neared the river. Now, it was right in front of her. Taking a deep breath, she took a huge step into it. She was mesmerised. She was alive! Her feet didn't feel anything, the only feeling she got was like standing in front of a heater. All around her, she saw rising green and orange flames and she also heard frantic shouts from Jay and Partha. She found that she was able to breathe the fire which was pretty queer. The river was very deep. She was slowly trying to swim upwards but was struggling quite a bit but swimming sideways wasn't much of a problem.

*

Jay was angry as well as shocked. So was Partha. But Natt remained calm. 'Who's next?'

'Have you gone nuts!' shouted Jay. 'You just killed my sister!'

Partha was too fumed to say anything. She had known something was wrong about this ghost all along.

'Don't worry. Your sister is alive.'

'Oh, don't be silly. How could she survive that river?'

Jay didn't know what to do. He, without a second thought, bolted straight into the river.

'JAY!' Partha yelled.

Jay didn't listen. In no time, he was there. Not stopping, he dived straight into the fire. He was quite surprised as he saw the fiery flames around him as if he was a fire-bender. There he saw Gita, trying to swim towards the other side. A wave of relief spread over his face and he also started to follow Gita.

'Gita!' he said in a muffled voice. 'We need to do our best to call Partha!'

Gita turned around and saw Jay. She simply nodded as she didn't want to risk speaking too much. Together, they started shouting.

*

Partha was the only one left. She was clueless of whether to enter by believing the ghost or not, after there was no reply from Jay and Gita. In fact, they were as good as dead at this point but the weird thing was she didn't see Jay or Gita's figures burn up. Then, she heard two voices. It was yelling her name, and the voice was familiar to Jay's and Gita's, though it was not clear.

'Partha…! We…alive!'

She was finally relieved, and ran into the fire followed by Natt. He didn't need any Emparon Dust, as he was already dead at least 200 years ago.

As Partha entered she saw Jay and Gita. 'Well that was a close call.'

They slowly swam towards the shore in the much denser lava. Finally, they reached the shore, panting while Natt was already waiting for them.

As the three came out of the water, they immediately fell down flat and hard on the ground as their energy had been completely drained. After a few minutes of silent resting, they slowly started getting up. Natt was waiting the entire time waiting for some acknowledgement. The three felt a bit embarrassed, with a little chuckle they said 'Sorry.'

Finally, they had crossed the River Of Flames, which was quite a big task, and they couldn't even think of what would have happened if Natt hadn't arrived on time. They would've just been waiting till someone came and rescued them, which was, in that place, impossible. Now, since they had crossed the river, they thought about what to do next.

'What should we do now?' asked Gita.

'Proceed I guess,' replied Partha.

Now, the three were staring at the face of Natt to get an answer. Even he remained quiet, as the place was filled with silence.

'Wait, aren't you our guide?' asked Gita.

'Yes,' Natt replied in a dragging voice.

'Then say where we should go.'

'Guys, I think you have got me wrong. Yes, I am a guide, but this still is your quest. If I hadn't come, you surely would have figured what to do by now, perhaps even earlier,' replied Natt.

'Fair point,' said Partha.

'Ok, so what we have done till now is following the dark clouds and the map. But we are almost there. Now, we have to figure out a new idea, to know where to go.'

Just as Partha finished speaking, Jay started to hear a voice. A cold voice.

'Trust your instincts Jay, Trust your mind. Even your closest may betray you. Trust your instincts.' were the words said. Jay was as quiet as ever, and his face went pale immediately. What was that voice? No one had talked, or sent signals except Stoming, though, this voice seemed different. Even if it was Stoming, he would now be determined in saving Nyra, and not texting into Jay's mind. But something was fishy. What did the words *'Even your closest may betray you'* mean? Gita and Partha wouldn't do such a thing. He could say that confidently. He hadn't met any single person recently except a ghost - Natt. Just as he was submerged into his thoughts, thinking hard, he just realised Gita was calling him non-stop.

'Jay!'

He regained his senses with a jerk. 'What's the matter?'

'None…just *thinking*,' he replied, quite shattered.

Nevertheless, they started to begin their long walk again. This seemed just the opposite. The three were walking in the front, and Natt was just following them. They felt more babysitted then guided into the dark side.

'I feel strange about that guy,' Jay whispered to the girls.

'Finally, someone understands me,' said Partha.

'Why do you feel that, Jay?' asked Gita.

'S-Someone…talked into my mind.'

The two were quite taken aback.

'It could be your imagination,' she said. 'It is common for people to have a corrupted mind at these times. Especially when you are about to walk into the centre of the dark side.'

Jay forced a chuckle. 'Yeah, that must be it.' However, he still couldn't stop thinking about it.' The voice seemed familiar, but not Stoming. Was it Az? Of course not. Only a sorcerer could talk into the minds of people, but Az, excluding all his power and skill, wasn't one. He just decided to distract his mind for some time.

Natt started to look angrier than before. He started dodging questions, and looked as if he was on to something. They walked and walked, they found nothing except the weather rapidly changing colder and colder. It was a shock for them, as till now, the weather was as hot as fire, whereas, it was turning just the opposite right now. It was not only cold, but also still. There were no winds, and the whole environment was lifeless.

'Are you sure we are going the right way?' asked Gita.

'To my knowledge, yes,' replied Partha.

Suddenly, he heard it again.

'No Jay, No.'

Chills ran down his spine. What was that? He ran towards Gita and Partha, and stopped them. Natt was sleep-floating, and looked as if he didn't have a clue of where he was going. Jay said the exact words the voice said to the two.

'What!' cried Gita.

'You heard it again?' asked Partha, this time more seriously.

'Yes…and I am sure it is not imagination,' replied Jay in a soft voice.

'He is supposed to guide us, and I'm not sure he is doing that right now,' said Partha.

'Guys, the map said this,' said Gita. 'It must be right. We've followed it and have come this far. That ghost might not be helping that much, I surely agree, but the map can't be wrong. Maybe it is better for us to keep moving on.'

Suddenly, they saw Natt glaring at them from behind.

'Why have you stopped?' he asked in a refreshed voice.

'Don't tell me he heard us.'

'Wait…what? What…heard you?' Natt became more vigilant.

'We stopped for a break,' managed Partha.

'Yes we did,' replied Jay.

'Very well…anyway, it must be getting cold for you...but not me!' Natt gave an awkward laugh, for what he called a joke.

'Ha…ha,' chuckled Jay with a pale face.

Natt scanned his surroundings a bit. 'You haven't reached the tree yet? Oh…you guys are really slow walkers.'

'What tree?'

'Oh…you will not be aware of it. *The tree of Ingress.'*

~CHAPTER FIFTEEN~

The Tree Of Ingress

'The tree of what?' asked Jay.

'That is the last barrier to the middle of the land of Phantoms. To say short, the gate to what you have come for.'

'Such a strange name for a tree,' said Gita.

'Ingress means entrance,' said Jay.

'Clever,' muttered Natt.

Jay grinned and stopped as Partha frowned. 'Anyway, the *Tree of Ingress*…What's that supposed to do?'

'You have to choose a fruit…...Out of the five. Bite the wrong fruit and you will be directly teleported to the place where you started…or worse. There are fruits which can even kill you,' explained Natt.

'Seems tough,' replied Jay.

'And scary,' added Gita.

'Anyway, we have not reached yet…so we have plenty of time to think about it.'

Everyone nodded and started walking a bit more. After some time, they spotted the tree. It was an unfathomably tall tree, with some branches almost scraping the dark clouds. It had long, strong prop roots dangling down to the ground, which made them guess it was at least five hundred years old. It had dense, purple leaves which were sparkling, and had very, very long branches. The roots extended till the place they were standing, and the tree could never be uprooted for sure. An advantage was that the tree didn't have life, otherwise they would have been kicked out, or strangled to death. The three stood in amazement, though Natt wasn't as surprised as the others were. She was sure that she could see the whole of Olympia from such a height. The purple leaves were the size of a school bag.

Jay walked towards the godly tree. 'This is the first, healthy tree which I have seen since I entered the dark side.'

Gita decided to look down, as she started to turn dizzy.

The three walked near and knelt down. They saw a few words neatly carved out on the bark. The cursive handwriting was pretty good, but it was a riddle again. They wondered, whoever wrote these words should have a love for poetry, as the words meant so much. At the same time, they were frustrated to figure out the meaning of the riddle each and every time they encountered something new.

'Another riddle!' said Partha, enthusiastically.

She wiped some dust out from the carved words and read:

You are standing in front of the Tree of Ingress,
Tall, strong and beautiful she is,
The correct fruit you have to guess and eat,
Otherwise you will miss your treat,
Different shapes and sizes they are,
But don't let the appearance fool you,
Oh, you have come this far,

You have engraved your name in the greatest few.

'It sounds more like a motivation,' said Jay.

'More like another clue,' replied Partha.

'Well, it's pretty obvious, isn't it?' said Gita. 'We have to eat a fruit ... the correct fruit, then, it will let us proceed further.'

'Can't we just ignore this thing?' asked Gita.

'Well, if you do not want to proceed, yes,' replied Natt.

The three thought again. If they didn't choose the correct fruit, they would face some dire consequences, and all this would end in vain.

'Guys I have a doubt,' said Jay. 'If we ourselves are struggling to move on, what about Thunder?'

'What do you expect? He's the leader of Olympia!' said Partha.

'First of all, If I get to rule Olympia, I would make it democratic.'

'Anyway, there are no people!' replied Gita.

'Guys! Be serious!' yelled Partha.

'Well, since the fruit is at such a height, we can't pluck it with our bare hands.'

'First, we have to think of deciding what fruit we are going to pluck,' said Jay.

'Guys, I think I know this,' said Gita.

She didn't say another word. She scanned every single fruit amongst the three. The first fruit was red, fat and looked extremely juicy. The second fruit was blue, and was not a bit bigger than a normal cherry. Though it was small, it was sparkling. The third fruit, also the last one, looked the brightest of all. It was golden, looked juicy, fat, and was glittering in the dark. She was composed and concentrated on every single fruit. The first two fruits looked normal to her eyes, when she started to look at the last fruit. The bright, golden one. You may think, the golden fruit would be the brightest of all, which would obviously prove it is the special one. But, she saw something different. She could see some figures slowly appearing on the fruit. It started to mean something to her. She, without having a second thought, shot the fruit with her arrow. Jay and Partha were surprised because Gita always talked to them before taking important decisions, but this was totally unlike her. The fruit fell down, gleaming with positivity. She luckily had her hands underneath it, as the fruit rested on her palms safely.

'Why did you do that?' asked Jay.

'Something felt right,' she said.

'What?'

'I could see a symbol fading in…that made me sure,' she said.

'Anyways, we got the fruit, what next?' Jay asked.

'You eat it,' replied Natt from behind. 'The riddle says after you pluck it, you eat it.'

'Guys…should I?' asked Gita, doubtfully.

'Ok…If you're sure,' said Jay.

She took a small bite of the fruit. The juiciness was really refreshing, as she felt something. Her eyes started to behave differently, and could see things she couldn't see before. She walked towards the bark without delay, and knelt down. She could see an opening, almost the size of a burrow, looking the same as the one they had seen before. She called the others, as they entered the burrow.

'Natt where-'

Jay called Natt to accompany them, though he was gone! They took a deep glance around and there was no sign of him. There are numerous possibilities of him vanishing into thin air, just like that, but the question was why did he leave them, without even saying? There was something tricky. Anyway, they had to carry on. Without bothering more about Natt, they entered the burrow.

'Why should everything end with a burrow?' asked Gita, crawling in.

'Yeah. I feel the same way,' replied Jay. He could hear his own echo in the empty space. They were wondering if they could find something gleaming, of course, *The Enchanted Book* inside this creepy burrow. Ah, if it were only that simple. They were looking for some kind of opening, so they could get out. It was also very difficult to breathe inside the cramped burrow. Finally, they could at least stand, as everything was just dark. Even the entry wasn't seen. They couldn't have come that far, just crawling but they had to admit that the dark side was prone to illusions and magic like these.

'I think we are stuck,' said Jay.

'I think we are there,' replied Partha, pointing at an opening, just two feet tall.

~CHAPTER SIXTEEN~

A Fight With The Dead

They were crawling towards the opening, as Gita stopped.

'What happened? Move on!' Jay's voice echoed from behind.

Without replying, she took her hand above the hole. She touched the mixture of dirt and clay, as she felt something embedded beneath the dirt. She wiped some of the dirt off and saw something that shocked her. 'This…is the same symbol which I had seen on the fruit.'

Partha and Jay were surprised too for a second. But for now, they felt getting out was more important. Gita hesitated a bit, but with Jay and Partha pressuring her to go through the opening, she had to go forward. She hesitantly crawled through the opening.

It turned scarier on the other side. The wind was slashing towards them, and there was no possibility of life, but they couldn't be very sure of ghosts.

Slowly, Jay and Partha got out and wiped the dust off their worn-out clothes. 'Creepy,' said Jay.

They fought the wind, as gusts of dust kept pushing them back. All of a sudden it stopped, which was a great relief for them. They walked further, as something swooshed past them.

'What was that?' Jay yelled.

'I saw it too. Everyone be alert-' Partha was about to finish, when they heard an eerie was behind them. It said,

'*No need to be alert.*'

They turned back and were stunned. It was Natt.

'Natt?' Jay asked.

'Yes of course,' he replied. His voice had turned deeper, and colder. It felt like he had turned more evil. His form was longer than before, and they could see his wicked eyes glittering with greed.

'Looks like you figured it out.'

'Yes ... we did,' replied Gita, shivering.

'*Bien*,' he replied in Spanish. Looking at the sudden transformation of Natt, they were speechless. *Where had he gone? How come he came back?* These thoughts were running in their mind continuously. But they decided not to ask him a word, because they were shaken up enough. They quietly followed the ghost, without uttering a single word. They walked for some time, and even Natt didn't speak anything, though he checked upon them every five minutes. Escaping wasn't an option here, and no doubt, Natt wouldn't let them escape.

'Wh ... Where are you taking us?' Gita forced herself to ask, when Natt let out the angriest yell.

'JUST FOLLOW ME!'

She just decided to shut her mouth and others didn't want to speak either. They followed him for a while, and finally stopped. Natt didn't say anything, but the environment turned colder. Suddenly, completely out of the blue, at least fifty more ghosts drifted down and surrounded them. They had no clue where the ghosts had come from. Every single ghost looked different. One was short and stout, and had lost an eye. They could almost see the hollow where the eye must have been there. The other one was taller, skinny, and had a hook as his wrist. His clothes were frayed, and looked scary. Another ghost looked decent. He was wearing a passable hat, and looked presentable (at least better than the other ghosts they had seen). But there was one thing in common for all the ghosts. All looked quite ancient. Bald, toothless you name it! They felt as though they were brought into an old age home, but only for ghosts. Frightened by the eerie looks, Jay, Gita and Partha slowly backed off. Who would not get scared after entering a land filled with old ghosts?

'*Looks like you brought them Natt,*' a grumpy voice said. It was another ghost from the crowd.

'*Yes I did,*' replied Natt.

'Master would be pleased!' another yelled. Natt grinned from ear to ear.

Natt looked at the three's confused faces. 'Well, children, I thought you were smart at first. I really did. But you proved me wrong. No ghost is kind to trespassers in the Land Of Phantoms. First it was the map. Oh, how naive you were to take it out in front of my eyes. All I had to do was summon a light gust of wind and poof! gone!'

A few ghosts chuckled. The three were starting to understand now.

'Then, it was the leaf. If you had known the value of the leaf, you wouldn't have given it away for your life. But, again, you give it to me as a gift!'

'What do you mean?' asked Gita. 'That is what the leaf was for!'

Natt smirked. 'The leaf could make ghosts vanish away for good when waved.'

The three were shocked. Such a powerful leaf and they simply gave it away.

Jay knew it. He knew Natt had been lying. The voices in his head were right. He wished he had trusted his senses before. Partha had a suspicion but he heard voices, which was the only truth they had at that time, even though he didn't know it. But what choice did they have? In no situation could the three have won. They could have either lost their way in the most dangerous part of Olympia or could have gotten led to an army of ghosts and got killed there. The only way they can escape is by killing the ghosts and getting the *Enchanted Book Of Resurrection* which sounded quite ridiculous, even to them.

Suddenly, there was a crash of lightning and thunder. The ghosts became immediately quiet and left a path. They bowed down silently, as the three could see a translucent, white and blue figure walking. It looked extremely strong, and a face as evil as Thunder. To their amusement, it also looked smarter.

'Who is that?' asked Gita.

Partha's face grew pale as she recognised the face from old scriptures and paintings. Her lips trembled. 'Frencher.'

Jay and Gita were appalled.

'Frencher? You mean, THE FRENCHER?'

'Well, yes,' replied Partha. 'The ghost of him at least.'

Had they ever known? A hike to Mt. St. Helena would take them to the most evil king of all time? Or meeting hundred servant ghosts?

Frencher stepped down and halted. He had a huge scar, translucent, silky hair, and was very handsome for a ghost. He had some armour on as well which had some faint inscriptions of ancient dialects. It was very difficult to read though as all his clothes were translucent.

Like all the other ghosts, there was only pure white smoke after his hips. He raised an eyebrow after seeing the three.

'*Who are they?*'

His voice was extremely deep and cold. He also sounded quite angry.

'*Thy highness…they are the three who have come to seek the-*' he looked at the three once more.

'*The Book.*'

'*Very well. . I guessed it at first sight,*' he replied, in the same creepy voice. He started circling the three with suspicion, as chills ran down their spine. Frencher stopped just in front of Jay, gave an eerie look, and then backed off. He raised an eyebrow and whispered something to Natt. He grinned and flew back again. Slowly, the ghosts started to surround the three, grinning from ear to ear. But Frencher still had the same serious expression.

He said-

'*Your quest cannot be fulfilled. .you better back off and never return in the future.*'

'Never,' said Jay. 'We won't leave without the book. You can't *scare* us. We have seen things weirder than you.'

'*Your choice. .I am giving you a chance to live, but you've chosen death,*' said Frencher.

'No,' repealed Jay. 'We have chosen to *fight.*'

He pulled his sword out of his scabbard furiously. Frencher was shocked. The blade, although it was dark and cold, glittered. The engraved 'F' still looked majestic, as Frencher's face turned from shocked to offended. He started to relive all his memories when he had the sword. He thought of how he had used it, whether for good and bad. He wept upon his memories, the degraded days, unworthy desires, and especially the day he cursed his loving daughters, though with no fault of their own. How much good could he have done with the sword? He realised it now. But his face shifted back to serious, and looked at the sword once more.

'That's my sword,' he said.

'Well it's mine now,' said Jay. This was another bullet straight into the heart for Frencher. He understood he really never deserved it.

'Bravery…That is what has brought you this far,' he said in a cold voice.

'But that's also going to be the cause of your demise.'

'Guards!' he yelled, as the fifty ghosts turned towards the three. It felt extremely spooky. 'KILL THEM!'

In less than a second, the ghosts began to swoop towards them at breakneck speeds. Jay slashed his sword to the left and right and so did Partha. Gita's bow and arrow were pretty useless, so she just tried dodging the attack.

'I wish I had a better weapon!' said Gita as she dodged another ghost.

Partha quickly threw a small dagger from her pocket. 'Here! Use this. I generally carry it along. But be careful, it's my mother's,' her voice became a bit more faint as she said this. Nevertheless, she continued slashing hard at the array of ghosts.

Gita smiled and started slashing at the ghosts as well. The first attack was finished. Now, it was just complete anarchy. The ghosts came and blindly attacked the three separately while Frencher was simply watching, waiting for his moment.

The only problem for the three was that the swords weren't doing much damage. It was like slicing through thin air. Some hits did cause a bit of a bruise but instantly healed.

Jay slashed his sword into a ghost, though there was a cut, it hardly took ten seconds to get healed again. The ghosts couldn't attack physically, though they entered his body and came out again which did give a bit of a shaky feeling to the body. It also made him feel weaker as the ghosts ate up a part of his energy. He tried and tried. He came to understand that he could never attack the ghosts, and the only thing he could do was defend himself. Gusts of dust and smoke erupted. Partha was trying to figure out a plan, at the same time, she tried to escape the ghosts. Jay snapped behind, dodged a ghost, and as he ran his sword into another one. He felt as if he was about to faint.

'We can't keep fighting these ghosts!' he yelled, panting. Frencher had his arms crossed and had an evil sneer.

Amongst the commotion Partha yelled at Frencher, 'You really are an evil father! We are trying to free your daughters from the curse you had cast mercilessly!'

Frencher thought again, and yelled, '*You still don't think I am here for my daughter do you? Those were days! Terrible days… And that curse is a deep cut in my heart which would never heal. But the past is the past. That is not my worry. I want to bring back my life.*'

'What?' Partha was stunned. Why did Frencher want to bring himself back? 'Wh…Why do you want to bring yourself back?' she asked quietly.

'*Thunder.*'

Suddenly, it all made sense.

'To kill him…To kill him with my own hands which are striving for revenge. If only his forefathers hadn't come I would have had my daughters…to myself.'

'Bu-But we are here to destroy him,' said Partha

'What? A trio of children killing Thunder? Impossible!'

'Give us the book, and we will destroy him,' she replied.

'I WILL KILL HIM! WITH MY OWN BARE HANDS! YOU ARE NO ONE TO STOP ME! GET OUT OF MY WAY!' he yelled as he cast a powerful spell into Partha. Gita and Jay were so busy fighting that they didn't see the exchange. Partha fell back and crashed into the ground. Even Gita and Jay couldn't bear it, and felt like they were going to faint anytime. Jay fell down to the ground. If a single ghost entered his body, he would surely lose his consciousness. Suddenly, they heard a thunderous sound. Lightning bolts crashed, as someone appeared from nowhere. They were sure the figure was a warrior. He had a sword in a scabbard, and was quite tall. The face was really familiar. It was Stoming. They were shocked. Stoming? How come he is here? He didn't speak anything as Stoming entered the scene and smiled at the three.

'Good that you have made it this far,' he said. His face was expressionless and didn't speak a word more. Frencher turned back, as he was shocked.

'You. The dog of Thunder.'

'Oh…thanks, *my king*,' replied Stoming. From this, it was sure that he hated Frencher too.

'You shouldn't be here!' yelled Gita, using her fading energy.

'Neither can I let you die,' replied Stoming, as he swung his sword. Bright, red energy attacked almost all the fifty ghosts swarming around him. Frencher smirked, and said -

'I am indeed impressed.'

The ghosts had a sharp jolt and fell back hard. Frencher just smiled.

'But I am sad...All these years and you still haven't learned!'

As he said this, his figure grew taller, as he started to groan in anger. Muscles erupted out his arm, and he looked at Stoming ferociously. Stoming was the centre of attraction. The ghosts recovered and swarmed around him but didn't attack him. They knew it was Frencher's fight. They were mere spectators and back-ups. Now, Gita and Jay had a chance. Partha knew it too. She recovered from Frencher's spell and ran up to Jay and Gita

'C'mon! It is our only chance!' she yelled.

She lifted Jay and Gita with her two arms, as they slowly started to feel better. They tip-toed away, in utter silence. In the meanwhile, Stoming was getting thrashed by Frencher. Here, Frencher was not getting inside Stoming, but was plainly smashing him. Stoming tried dodging him and counter attacking, but it was in vain. The other ghosts were also going through him from time-to-time, draining his energy. Overall, it looked as if Stoming had entered hell willingly. The three avoided looking at Stoming, and tried sneaking away from the behind of a huge rock, without getting spotted. But Jay couldn't bear it like always. He was almost in tears, seeing Stoming sacrificing himself for them.

'We have to go save him!' he whispered to the two.

'What?' replied Partha. We just escaped!'

'Well, if we go and try killing Frencher, we would get killed and it would totally defeat the purpose why Stoming was fighting for them,' said Gita.

'Exactly,' said Partha. 'Jay, be honest, do you really think you can kill Frencher?'

'No…Bu-but we should at least try and save him…we can't let a man die for us,' replied Jay.

'If we go and fight him, we don't have any other chance to get the book,' said Gita.

Jay agreed, though he was still extremely worried about Stoming. At the same time he had started to build confidence that Stoming would get through Frencher.

'Okay.'

They sneaked away behind the rock, and ran straight without looking back. They ran for about two hundred metres, though they couldn't see anything related to the book.

Finally, they stopped. They could see the book kept on a bark, with at least ten skulls placed around them. It added more eeriness to the environment. The three were clueless, and Jay carelessly walked near the book.

'STOP!' yelled Partha.

'What…Why?' asked Jay.

'There must be some sort of protection. The last time you got the book, you ran into a teleporter. The last time Thunder got the book, we heard he met some kind of godly man,' she explained.

'What about Frencher?' Jay asked. 'We just fought him and almost died.'

'There must be something greater than Frencher…'

'Guys…I just realised something,' said Gita. 'We haven't really thought about whom we would bring back after getting the book.'

'Well, our main goal was to stop Thunder from getting the book, not using it,' replied Jay.

'Maybe the book would only be accessible if we have someone in mind,' said Partha.

'Then, if Thunder tried to get the book, he can't, right?' asked Gita.

'Who knows, Thunder *might* have someone to bring back,' replied Partha.

'So…who do we have to bring back?'

'I think I know,' said Jay. He looked at the others and smiled. They understood.

'*Lashman*,' they said together. They shut their eyes tight, and only thought of Lashman's complexion that Brej described.

Astonishingly, light started gleaming on The Enchanted Book, same as it shined in the burrow two and a half years ago. Jay gently opened his eyes, wondering if it had worked. The light of the book had lightened up the whole environment.

'Whoa!' exclaimed Jay.

Partha and Gita opened their eyes, and were also surprised to see the book. They all felt gleeful. How many obstacles had they faced to get this single book! They held their hands and started laughing in joy. They noticed the book, as it slowly started to rise! It floated on the log, and ponderously hovered to their hands.

'Guys ... we just got *The Enchanted Book of Resurrection*.'

'What about Stoming?' asked Jay. Their faces slowly dimmed. Now, they felt really bad for leaving Stoming amidst a hundred ghosts, and letting him fight on his own. They could only pray he had escaped, or at least alive in a place safe and sound.

'C'mon! We have to take the book to a safer place!' yelled Partha.

Even before they had studied the book well, they heard something. They turned back, and were stunned. It was a stampede. It was a stampede of ghosts, racing towards them outrageously.

'RUN!' yelled Gita, as the three started running as fast as they could. The ghosts were picking up speed, and it looked like they were going to die for sure considering the weakness of the three. They tried their best and made it to the spot where they left Stoming. They hoped for Stoming to lay in wait for them but shocking, he wasn't there!

'Where is Stoming?' cried Jay.

'Huh. That's strange. There is not even a trace of him.' Partha noticed. 'Unless ...'

'No. I don't want to even think of that.' declared Gita.

Jay was too shocked to say anything. Right now, he had to stay alive. The ghosts were nearing them by the second. They could travel much faster than the three. Suddenly, a figure appeared a small distance away from them. The three really hoped it was Stoming, but it was Brej and Asha! For some reason, they were yelling and signalling the three to come to their spot.

'I think they want us to follow them,' observed Partha

Jay and Gita agreed and went in the direction where Asha and Brej were waving. The ghosts simply followed Jay, Partha and Gita too.

Asha and Brej were now insanely close to Jay, Gita and Partha and so were the ghosts.

The voices of Brej was clearly audible. 'Touch this on the count of three!' He was pointing to a glowing ball which resembled Az's teleporter.

'One, two, three!' Brej shouted as Jay, Gita and Partha dived as they made contact with the teleporter in the nick of time. Partha held the book in one hand and touched the teleporter with another as it turned all quiet. The smoky uncomfortable smell was gone, the sky was orange mixed with a little purple as it was evening time. They were standing on a ground with a bit of yellow grass here and there. Rain was drizzling, as the fresh water tickled the face of Jay. A few insects were chirping, and a huge, run down castle stood far away from them. There were a couple of trees around them, the size of banyan and peepal trees with prop roots hanging for extra support. Jay and Gita saw their mother more clearly this time and in less than a second, they were wrapped in a warm embrace. They felt grateful that they could be with their mother again despite almost losing her for the second time. Asha wiped a tear off her eyes as the embrace ended. Partha and Brej simply smiled at the touching moment. They were feeling pretty ravenous even though the Land Of The Phantoms reduced the feel of hunger. Just as Jay wiped the mud off his shoulder, he could see quite a large, cosy hut, with smoke drifting out the chimney leisurely. They heard voices inside the hut, and they were eager to go in.

After calming down a bit, Brej noticed the book in Partha's hand.

'You got the book!'

The three smiled in satisfaction.

'Have you thought about who you were going to resurrect?'

Gita nodded. 'Yes, but that's for later,' she said. 'Anyway where are we?'

Everyone looked at the house.

'Ahh…I haven't seen this place in such a long time,' said Brej with a sigh.

~CHAPTER SEVENTEEN~

Outbreak Of Emotions

A couple of metres before them stood a house. I didn't look that advanced but enough for a cosy and safe home. It had cement walls in the house which were relatively clean and a wooden door at the front. It had a couple of glass windows here and there. The house was at least ten feet in height.

'This brings back many memories,' said Partha.

Brej started walking towards the house. 'Let's go inside.'

The others followed him and walked to the door and opened it as it made a screeching sound. The house inside was quite simple and normal but spacious. It had a pathway leading to the living room. On the side of the pathway, there was a small bathroom. The living room had a small sofa which looked quite comfy. The floor was wooden with a few cracks around the corner. On the two sides of the living room, there were two bedrooms for a good night's sleep.

'Not bad,' muttered Jay.

'Yes,' agreed Gita. 'Pretty neat home for a place under Thunder's control.

Partha was looking at a few portraits which showed her, her father and mother smiling. 'When was this?'

Brej came near Partha. 'I remember. I was the one that took this photo.'

There was a door in the living room Jay noticed. 'Is this the dining room?'

'Yeah,' said Partha.

Jay opened it and saw something he never expected.

'Want a cup of tea?' a voice asked. It was Stoming.

Bingo and the cousins were there as well, sipping on tea!

'This tea tastes really good,' said Sara.

Jay ran and gave Stoming a big hug which almost made Stoming drop his tea cup.

'Whoa…Someone is energetic.'

'Where were you?' questioned Jay.

'Well, I fought the ghosts, and as I came to know that Frencher was not going to give up, I pushed them back a bit and teleported back here,' answered Stoming.

Gita was too shocked as well and followed Jay. She and Jay went to Bingo and the cousins to catch up a bit. Bingo was very relieved that his children were alive and in good health. He squeezed them so hard, they almost popped like a balloon. 'I am so glad you are alive.'

'Yes, dad. Us too,' said Jay, his voice hoarse from the bone-crushing they had got from their father.

Partha came into the dining room and hugged Nyra and Az with tears in her eyes. Nyra was still quite weak but she felt way better knowing that her daughter was safe and sound and in her arms. Az too felt the same way.

'What happened? How did you-' Partha was speechless.

'It's a long story,' replied Az.

Partha simply didn't reply in shock and sat down in an empty chair. There were at least four chairs remaining which were on a pile near the corner of the dining room. There was a huge dining table in the centre with chairs surrounding it where everybody was sitting. There was a small path which led to the kitchen which had a wooden counter and a stove at the centre of the counter. Asha slowly walked into the kitchen to fetch a cup of tea, as she was stunned again. She saw Bingo. Her own husband, whom she had missed for fifteen long years. They hugged with tears, as everyone sat for dinner. It had been quite an emotional roller-coaster and all they needed right then was a nice, joyful dinner with their families.

'It's quite nice, isn't it?' said Bingo, his spirits quite high. 'To have everybody back.'

Stoming nodded. 'Let's have a toast. To the reunited families and friendships,' he said. 'Cheers!'

Everyone raised and brought their mugs together. 'Cheers!'

Gita noticed Brej's long face as she brought her mug back down. She immediately understood. 'Reminding myself…' She went into the living space to fetch the book. She came back in less than ten seconds to the surprised faces of Bingo, Stoming, Az and Nyra.

'The book!' cried Bingo.

'You got it!' said Stoming. 'Now,' he faced his chair towards Gita. 'Who's it going to be?'

Jay and Partha got up from their chairs and walked up to Gita. Together, they held the book with Gita in the middle. 'Lashman,' they said and once again tried picturing his face based on the descriptions given by Brej. Brej immediately got up from his seat in shock. Was he really going to see his long lost friend again? The book began emitting light and shaking in the arms of the three. The light was also mixed with a blue hue which intensified the process even more. Stoming, Bingo and Brej moved out of the way as the book started creating a human figure in front of them, almost like a hologram projector. It only took a few seconds for the hazy figure, made out of light, to transform into the live body of the clueless Lashman. He was a tall, good-looking man. But other than that, he was pretty grim. His hair was messed up and his face was pale. It seemed that the resurrection had taken a serious toll on him. Brej's face lit up as he immediately went and hugged Lashman before the latter even knew if he existed or not.

'Lashman! You are back!' cried Brej.

Lashman needed time to process this. For him, just a moment ago, Thunder had stabbed him with his sword and next second, he was being hugged by his close friend. And who were the other people? Were his eyes playing a trick or were the three children holding an Enchanted Book? He just had so many questions.

Meanwhile, hesitantly, Stoming came to face Lashman. He simply forgot all his questions but only remembered the reason for his troubles. 'Stoming. What is this traitor doing here?' He immediately lunged at Stoming who tried to push him away without hurting him. Brej swiftly pulled Lashman away who was still quite enraged. 'Ok. You have a lot to catch up on.'

Stoming simply decided to walk away to prevent any problems. It was quite clear that he had made a lot of enemies.

'The only thing I want to catch is that man,' yelled Lashman.

Brej used all his power to push Lashman into a chair.

'What is this-' Lashman was about to ask when he noticed the faces of Bingo and Asha. 'Wait…is that-?'

'Yes,' said Brej. He understood.

'Where am I?' shouted Lashman. It sounded like he was losing his mind. 'The last time I saw these people, one had gone into hiding and one was in Thunder's dungeon.' He clutched his head and fell back onto the chair.

Bingo and Brej went and went to Lashman's aid. Clearly, the resurrection had taken a toll on his mental state as well.

'Ok. We have a lot of explaining to do,' said Brej. 'First of all, yes, they are Bingo and Asha,' he pointed at them. 'And these two are their children,' he pointed at Jay and Gita.

'Wait-' said Lashman. 'The children? THE children?'

'Yep,' replied Brej. 'The first book was stolen from them by Thunder, thanks to the "insider",' Lashman understood and turned to scowl at Stoming who was hiding in the corner of the room. 'But they got it back and tore it, to destroy Thunder's scepter. Unfortunately, they weren't able to get the Book Of Knowledge for long as Thunder took it back. Now they have managed to get the Book Of Resurrection and they chose you to revive.'

'I do accept the gesture,' said Lashman. 'But why this man?' he pointed at Stoming, in the corner. 'He did betray you, didn't he?'

'Well, then Thunder betrayed him so he joined us and has guided and aided us quite well,' said Jay.

Now, it was just a matter of clarifying the entire situation to Lashman. Boy, had he missed a lot. Everyone, even Stoming started pitching in and told the entire story of Olympia and their lives: how they had got the books, their journey to the castle of Thunder, how they rescued Partha and then Jay, Partha and Gita described the unheard story of how they crossed the Land Of the Phantoms, met Brej and Asha and all of the little but fearful adventures they had in between.

Once they had finished, Lashman had regained his senses. He finally began to remember the past events of his life. It seemed all it needed was a story session to regain his memories and sanity.

'Well, you know what they say,' said Brej. 'Never trust a ghost.'

Lashman didn't say anything but simply went to Brej and whispered something in his ear.

Brej's face grew grimmer. 'No, didn't find her. Couldn't do much.'

'Who,' asked Stoming.

'Aanya,' replied Brej, in a very dejected and monotonous tone. 'Lost in the war. First, it was my parents, then it was my wife…'

Jay, Bingo and Gita immediately popped up after hearing the mention of Aanya.

'Wait,' said Jay. 'Aanya? Are you sure you aren't saying your name wrong?'

'What do you mean? It's my wife,' replied Brej. 'How can I say her name wrong?'

Jay was seriously speculating the situation. He was almost sure he was right. But then, there is that awkward situation where he isn't. He turned to Gita and Bingo and they simply nodded like they knew it for sure.

Jay was a bit more convinced now. He simply looked at Stoming and signalled him for the teleporting.

Stoming saw his signal. '*Why?*' he mouthed.

'*Just do it*,' Jay mouthed back.

Stoming nodded and began channelling his inner energy. Suddenly blue sparks started shooting out of his body. His eyes flashed blue as Brej, Lashman, Asha and the cousins looked at him, amazed.

'What is he doing?' asked Lashman, suddenly suspicious.

Jay immediately went and whispered something in Stoming's ear.

One could see a faint smile on Stoming's face.

'Oh, you'll see,' said Gita. 'Brej, you are going to love this.'

~CHAPTER ELEVEN~

An Appalling Find

Everyone was teleported in a large chamber of pure, blue light. They were teleported to an area in the outskirts of San Francisco. The light was fading and when they looked up, they could see the typical evening sky on Earth, with pinkish blue clouds covering the sky and the faint outline of a crescent moon could be seen as well. The ground had some fresh, green grass and there was a thin metalled road a few metres in front of them. When they turned around, they saw a dingy but comfortable wooden cottage. A couple of lush, evergreen trees surrounded it. There were even some cottages, they could spot in the distance. Stoming had pretty much transfigured himself into a normal, middle aged man, as the last thing he wanted was to get spotted and arrested by the police on earth.

Lashman looked around, pretty confused. 'Where are we?'

Brej understood the atmosphere and the sky. Even though he had been hiding in the Land Of The Phantoms for fourteen years, he could remember these conditions at the back of his head. 'Earth. But where on Earth?'

Jay dragged Brej in excitement to the front door of the cottage and rang the bell vigorously.

'What are you doing?' asked Brej.

Jay didn't reply and just waited for the door to open. By then, everyone rushed to Jay's side to see what the excitement was all about. Brej was still clueless why Jay had yanked him all the way from Olympia to a small, normal suburban house. Jay quickly gestured to everyone except Brej to move aside. They nodded and went towards the back of the house.

Finally the door was opened by a fourteen year old teenager who looked pretty worn out. Still, his confusion wasn't hidden. 'Uh…Jay? Why are you here? Who is he?

'I just wanted to pay a visit. This is my…uncle. He just wanted to come along.'

Zen looked pretty perplexed but was happy to oblige. 'Well come in.'

Brej had his eyes fixed on the boy, as Jay guided him to the couch.

'Zen! Who's at the door?' they heard Zen's mom, followed by a clank of several steel vessels. She walked into the living room and saw Brej. First, her expression was quite normal as she didn't recognise him immediately. But Brej recognised her immediately.

'Aanya?' Brej's face was filled with joy. He knelt on his knees, and started sobbing. Aanya, with her brown eyes full of tears ran towards Brej, who was weeping and pulled him up. They hugged each other tightly, remembering all the memories they had many years ago.

Zen was absolutely clueless on what was happening. 'Mom who's th-'

Even before he could finish, Brej came and gave him a tight bear hug. By then, the others outside the house started knocking on the front door to see what all the commotion was about. Jay silently went to the door and let them in. The door pretty much burst open and Stoming, Az, Nyra and Lashman were surprised to find Brej, Aanya and Zen sitting on the couch.

'Aanya!' cried Az. Then, he looked at Jay in shock.

Jay simply smiled back. 'It's a small world.'

Lashman too was overjoyed for his friend and went to meet and catch up with Aanya.

When Aanya saw the face. Stoming, she scowled.

Stoming noticed it. 'God, did I really make that many enemies? I am not here to kill you now, for goodness sake.'

Aanya looked at Brej. Brej just nodded.

Zen was still pretty appalled and clueless. 'Who is he?' he cried.

'He's your *father*,' said Aanya.

Zen was shocked. *His dad was alive?* The poor boy had never ever seen his dad, his mother had only told him that his father had died before he was born.

He went to Jay for an explanation. 'How did you find him?'

'Well, the only thing I am going to say is, Olympia is real. You can ask your dad for more details.'

Zen simply nodded and ran off to his newly reunited family.

The family embraced joyously, when Bingo put an arm around Jay and Gita. Even Stoming was quite emotional, but not as much as the others. Brej was going to stay with Zen and his mom. So was Lashman, as it was quite dangerous for him to go back to Olympia and risk being seen and killed by Thunder. Besides, he was still pretty weak. After some time, Stoming teleported everyone to the untouched Ramsay residence.

'Well, I guess Thunder didn't destroy your house,' said Partha. 'Who knows what his plan is.'

Stoming then went on to teleport with Az, Nyra and Partha back to Az's house in Olympia.

Sara shook off some dust off her legs. 'Well, we might as well go in.'

Asha felt nostalgic. The memory of this house was still fresh in her memories. She remembered everything from the blue paint to the traditional pulley doorbell.

Bingo looked at Asha and smiled. 'Do you remember?'

'Oh, how could I forget,' replied Asha.

Arjun and Tara, who remained silent when a lot of drama was unfolding around them, started gaining their usual talkative sense.

Bingo went and opened the door of his house only to find the shock of his life. His couches were torn and the carpet had many tiny crumbs scattered all over it. The tables were tipped over and the house looked like it was destroyed by a tornado.

'Well, this is not how I remembered this house,' said Asha, getting a very bad first impression of the neatness of the house.

Arjun looked around, appalled. 'Is there anyway Thunder wreaked havoc only in the inside of the house?'

'Well, it certainly looks like it,' replied Gita.

Suddenly they heard many screeches and barks. In less than a second, they were almost stampeded by a single golden retriever.

'Cookie!' cried Tara. 'How could we forget you?'

Jay immediately took the half infuriated, half joyous Cookie into his hands and started scratching it comfortingly under his jaw. Immediately, the others came and started petting Cookie, feeling pretty dejected that they didn't take him to Olympia along with them.

Asha gave a bewildered look to Bingo. 'Who is this?' she asked. 'I thought you didn't like pets.'

She loved dogs but never remembered getting one.

'Well,' replied Bingo. 'People change.'

Asha came and pet Cookie for the first time along with the others.

Suddenly, everyone heard a loud noise. It sounded like a sudden blast of wind and it was coming just outside their house. After a few seconds, it immediately became faint. After that, all that could be heard was the hooting of an owl. Jay quickly ran out and saw Polskite, the owl standing outside. Once Polskite saw Jay, he flew right onto Jay's shoulder.

After a sudden jerk, Jay smiled. 'Stoming…'

THE END

www.ingramcontent.com/pod-product-compliance
Lightning Source LLC
LaVergne TN
LVHW010555160826
845677LV00013B/3138

* 9 7 9 8 8 4 6 6 8 7 1 9 6 *